1

Book 2

Kylie and the Quokkas
of
Rottnest Island

Jonathan Macpherson

Rotto!
Book 2
Kylie and the Quokkas
of
Rottnest Island

Jonathan Macpherson
Copyright © 2018 by Jonathan Macpherson.
All Rights Reserved.

For Caio, Bianca & Annie.

Chapter 1

Kylie and her mum got out of their car, both squinting in the early morning sun. It was only 8:00am but it already felt warm. There was a ferry boat tied to the dock, the biggest boat Kylie had ever seen. The boat was going to take her and her class to Rottnest Island, a beautiful island paradise just off the coast of Western Australia. Kylie had never been, but she had heard so much about "Rotto," as the people from her hometown of Perth called it, and she was incredibly excited to be going for the first time.

She looked around at the other cars parking nearby, children streaming out of them, flocking towards the ticket station on the quay where their teacher, Miss Taylor, was sorting them into two lines and taking attendance.

Kylie's mum leant over her and put some sunscreen on her face.

"I've put sunscreen on already, Mum," Kylie said.

"Yes, but you might have missed a few spots." Her mum made sure every part of her face, neck and ears were safely covered, while Kylie watched in amusement as the Toohey Twins, who were boy/girl twins and were always causing little accidents of one kind or another, stood by their mum's car. Sam, the boy, tried to give Sarah a piggyback. He was having great difficulty as both he and Sarah were wearing their backpacks. He couldn't quite bear the weight and staggered backwards against their car, immediately being told off by their mother.

"Now remember," Kylie's mum said, "quokkas are wild animals. Don't get too close to them, they could hurt you."

"Okay," Kylie said, wrapping her arms around her mum's waist.

"And don't stray far from Miss Taylor, especially when you're swimming. You know you're not very good in the water."

"Okay. Bye, Mum."

"Bye, darling. Have a great day!" her mum said, then kissed her cheek. Kylie ran to join the other kids, her hat falling off and dangling down her back by the strap. "Kylie, keep your hat on," her mother called, "it's going to be very hot!"

Kylie pulled her hat back on and waved to her mother.

"Keep your hat on, Kylie" a mocking voice echoed behind her. She didn't need to turn around; she knew it was Danny Wilson, the meanest boy in her class. Danny had a talent for saying nasty things and he seemed to enjoy saying them to Kylie more than all the other kids in grade three. She looked over her shoulder to see him smiling broadly in a horribly sarcastic way. But then he stopped, his smile changing to a look of concern. He turned away and put his school bag on the ground, tending to something inside it.

Kylie dashed over to the line in front of Miss Taylor and the assistant teacher, Mrs Phelps. Miss Taylor was young, rosy–cheeked and full of enthusiasm, and Mrs Phelps was kindly and reminded Kylie of her grandmother. Wondering what had distracted Danny, Kylie turned to see him still leaning over his bag. He jerked back suddenly, as if he'd had a nasty surprise, then zipped the bag shut smartly. He picked it up and carried it by his side, holding it away from his leg as he approached the back of the line. Kylie hoped someone else would arrive before he did, so she wouldn't have to put up with him.

"Hi Kylie" said her classmate Charlie, big eyes smiling through his thick–rimmed glasses.

"Hi Charlie," she said, "you're just in time!"

He noticed Danny coming and nodded at her, understanding just what she meant.

"I can't believe we're finally going to Rottnest Island!" she said.

"Have you ever been before?" he asked.

"No, this is my first time," Kylie replied.

"I go to Rotto all the time with my family. I'll show you round," he said excitedly, flashing his gap-toothed smile. The class had been planning the trip for months and the students had been marking off the days on the class calendar.

"Kylie," Miss Taylor called, "how would you like to be class leader today?"

"Um, I'm not sure, Miss Taylor," Kylie said.

"It's an important job," her teacher said, handing Kylie a pen and a clipboard with the class list on it. "I'll need you to go around the class and check that everyone is present. Not all day, just every now and then, like when we're swimming, at lunch, and before we take the ferry home. I might ask you to run a couple of little errands too. Do you think you can manage all that?"

"I think I'd better not, Miss Taylor," she said.

"Why not?"

"Well, I'm sure I'll probably lose the list or make a mistake, or something. Maybe you should ask Charlie to do it." Lately, Kylie had been losing or misplacing things, whether it was her water bottle or a hat, or just about anything, and she had started to feel like a bit of a "clumsy wumsy," as some of her classmates had put it.

"Okay, then. Charlie, would you like to be class leader?"

"Oh, yes, Miss Taylor!"

"Very good," she said. Kylie felt slightly sad as she handed the clipboard and pen to Charlie. Miss Taylor stuck a bright gold "Class Leader" sticker on Charlie's shirt and he beamed with pride.

"Maybe next time, Kylie?" Miss Taylor asked with a smile. Kylie nodded. She was very fond of Miss Taylor, even though she seemed to have a mild case of what Kylie's mum called MDA, short for "Mobile Device Addiction". Kylie often caught Miss Taylor on her phone in class, her finger flicking up and back as she scrolled over her social media apps. But that was only when the class was having quiet time. When she was teaching, Miss Taylor was one hundred percent focused on the children, and they all thought she was the best teacher in the school.

Soon almost the entire class was present, except for the Toohey Twins.

"Look out!" called Charlie, and Kylie turned to see the pig-gy-backing twins floundering towards her, out of control. Sarah was carrying Sam, but was close to falling on her face. Fortunately she swayed to one side and fell backwards, their backpacks acting like airbags and cushioning the fall as they hit the deck.

"Sarah Toohey is present!" called Sarah, with her hand in the air.

Sam, lying hidden beneath Sarah's backpack, stuck his arm in the air, his muffled voice calling "Sam Toohey is also here!" and the class erupted into uncontrollable giggles.

Miss Taylor did her best not to smile and after sternly warning the twins to curb their shenanigans, she and Mrs Phelps led the way onto the ferry and up to the top deck.

Chapter 2

Kylie and Charlie found an empty booth by the window and sat opposite each other.

"I brang lots of snacks," Charlie said.

"I brought some too," said Kylie.

"But I got *lots!*" he said, unzipping his backpack, which was full to the brim with potato chips, crackers, chocolate chip cookies, cheese sticks and lollies.

"Wow," Kylie said, looking in awe.

"If you get hungry, just let me know," he said.

Suddenly a pair of hands shot inside the bag and started rifling through the snacks, taking as many as they could gather. No surprise–it was Danny. "Oh, I don't like Burger Rings," he said, shoving the packet back inside and pulling out a different one. "Ah, perfect."

"Put them back!" snapped Kylie.

"He just said he wants to share," Danny said.

"He didn't say you could take whatever you want!"

"Course he did," Danny said.

"Don't worry, Kylie, it's okay," Charlie said, friendly as ever.

"See?" Danny said. "Didn't your parents teach you to share?" Danny asked, a smirk on his face. Kylie crossed her arms and frowned furiously. "Shove over then, don't take up the whole seat!" Danny said, sliding beside her. She turned and gazed out over the water below, glittering with sunlight. It was so beautiful she soon forgot about the nuisance sitting beside her.

The engines roared and the boat pulled away from the dock. The whole class was buzzing with excitement as they steered out past the red and white lighthouse and out to the brilliant dark blue sea. The ferry was so big it cut through the waves and Kylie noticed Rafa, who everyone agreed was the smartest boy in the class, standing upright without rocking in the slightest. Kylie wondered why he was standing up and staring over the side. She soon got her answer.

"Look!" Rafa exclaimed, and everybody looked down to see a pod of dolphins swimming alongside the ferry. Even Danny was entranced as the dolphins leapt out of the water and dived back in. Then, abruptly, they pulled away in another direction.

"Like animals, do ya?" Danny asked with a wry smile.

"Everyone likes dolphins," Kylie said.

"Take a look at this," Danny said, and pulled the zip of his backpack slightly open. "Can you see him?"

"No," Kylie said, wondering what she was supposed to be looking at. It was dark inside. Then Danny opened it a little more and a mouth full of sharp teeth pushed out, hissing. Kylie and Charlie flinched back and Danny laughed as the animal wriggled its snout further out so its green eyes were showing. It was an orange cat. But not your average household cat. Judging by its head, this was a very large, wild cat–not the kind you keep as a pet. Danny pulled the top of the bag up, covering the animal, and zipped it shut.

"Why did you bring that?" Kylie asked.

"It's a stray. Kept coming to our place to play with our cat and steal its food. My dad was going to take it to the vet today to have it put to sleep. So I rescued him. I'm going to free him on Rottnest Island."

"That doesn't sound like a good idea," Kylie said.

"Why not? You think I should just let them kill him?" Danny snarled.

"Well, what if it kills a bird or something?"

"That's nature for ya. Dogs eat cats. Cats eat birds."

"Dogs don't eat cats," Kylie said.

"Course they do! Don't you watch nature shows on TV?" Danny smirked.

Kylie didn't bother arguing. She was more concerned about the stowaway cat. "And your parents don't know about this?"

"Nobody knows, except you two. So don't tell anybody."

"I think you should tell the teacher," Charlie said.

"I'm not telling anyone and neither are you. See this?" he turned his forearm over and showed them a nasty scratch wound. It was scabbed over, but it was clear it had been pretty deep. "The cat did that. If you tell anyone about him, I'll set him onto you. You got it?"

"Okay," Charlie said nervously. "Just...keep it away from me, please."

Chapter 3

A
s they drew closer to Rottnest the anticipation built, noisy chatter among the students. Kylie looked down in amazement at the beautiful, clear turquoise water, that stretched all the way to the island's white, sandy beaches. The engines eased to a hum as they pulled close to the jetty.

"This is Thomson Bay," Charlie said, as the boat swung around to dock.

"Welcome to Rottnest Island," came the Captain's voice over the loudspeakers, "have a pleasant stay."

They watched the crew in their smart, white uniforms as they tied the ferry to the dock with the thickest ropes Kylie had ever seen. When the engines stopped, Miss Taylor led them downstairs and over the gangplank and soon they were on the jetty, standing in line again.

"Everyone here, Charlie?" asked Miss Taylor.

"Yes, Miss Taylor," Charlie said, having already done a head count twice over.

"Well done," she said, then looked at Mrs Phelps, who gave her a little nod of confirmation. "Okay, let's go!" Miss Taylor said cheerfully.

As they walked off the jetty up towards the faded orange seawall, Kylie took a deep breath in through her nose, delighting in the scents of wild flowers and wattle trees mixed with the fresh sea air. They followed the winding path past the busy visitor centre, and up around the seawall, where they were greeted by the cutest animals Kylie had ever seen: quokkas. To Kylie, they looked like baby kangaroos, (known as joeys), crossed with teddy bears. Three of the furry little creatures sat beneath a tree eating leaves.

Edging closer and closer to the incredibly friendly animals, which didn't seem to mind in the slightest, the children made the kind of noises you would expect from children when they see adorable animals. Kylie was not the only one who felt a desperate urge to cuddle at least one of them.

"Now remember, no touching the quokkas, and definitely no feeding them," Miss Taylor said to the class.

"They look a bit like joeys!" Kylie said.

"That's a good observation, Kylie," said Miss Taylor. "They are marsupials, so, just like kangaroos, they carry their babies in a pouch."

"They're just so cute!" Kylie said.

"Aw, so cutie wootie," Danny mocked. Kylie just ignored him. Miss Taylor and Mrs Phelps took several photos of the class with the quokkas.

"Okay, who wants to go for a swim?" Miss Taylor asked.

"Me!" everyone answered in a chorus.

"Alright, we'll go to Pinky Beach, just over by the lighthouse," she said, pointing at the lighthouse on top of a small hill. They headed along a path lined with overhanging trees which shaded them as they passed several old cottages, a few more friendly quokkas, and even a magnificent peacock, which strutted across their path, barely noticing them.

The Toohey twins did their best quokka imitations, hopping along and bumping heads, and bumping each other over, before they all arrived at the glorious white beach below the lighthouse, which towered above them, stretching far into the blue sky. The turquoise water was crystal clear. They put their bags on the beach and kicked off their shoes. Miss Taylor and Mrs Phelps made sure everyone had plenty of sunscreen on.

Mrs Phelps pointed to a mound of rock that rose out of the water quite a way out from shore and told them it was the nest of a sea eagle, or osprey, and it had been built by the bird's ancestors over a hundred years ago. They gazed in wonder, hoping to see the bird, but it didn't appear.

Before long they had forgotten their disappointment and were swimming in the shallow water, jumping and diving and splashing about, and having plenty of fun. Kylie noticed some of the kids diving and frolicking in deeper water, and thought it looked like so much fun. But she didn't dare stray from Miss Taylor's side.

"Stingray!" called Charlie, and they all turned to see a flat, black shadow beneath the water zooming away from the group. Danny shrieked and ran ashore, along with a few of the other kids.

"They won't hurt you," Miss Taylor said, but there was no convincing some of the students.

"They can kill you!" Danny said.

"They won't even come near you," Mrs Phelps said, sounding slightly annoyed that Danny had caused a minor panic.

Danny felt humiliated and stayed on the beach while the other kids played in the water.

The twins were at it again, this time seeing who could do a handstand the longest. But they didn't get to find out, as a big wave struck, tumbling them over and washing over them, much to everyone's amusement.

Kylie and Charlie played in the water for some time then went and sat on their towels and dried off.

Charlie handed Kylie a bag of Cheezels while he grabbed a packet of Twisties, his favourite snack. Kylie noticed some seagulls appearing around them.

"Like a snack?" Charlie asked Danny, who was sitting nearby. He scowled and shook his head.

"Put your hat on, Kylie," mocked Danny, in a silly voice that was supposed to sound like her mother. She frowned at him and refused to put it on, purely out of spite. She and Charlie opened their treats and were munching away when Kylie noticed a young quokka nearby, staring longingly at them.

"I think he wants one," said Charlie.

"But you mustn't, remember?" Kylie reminded him.

"I know," said Charlie. "But he looks so friendly."

Charlie took out a Twistie, then gasped, marvelling at its size. "It's a record!" he said.

"Wow!" Kylie said. "What a beauty! It's as long as your hand!"

Charlie's smile was just as big as the Twistie, and as he brought it towards his mouth, something flashed over his shoulder, and he bit fresh air–the Twistie was gone! He looked around in bewilderment, then saw Danny falling back on the sand laughing. He took another Twistie, and before he could get it into his mouth, another flash, and gone.

"The seagulls!" Kylie said, and they looked up to see four or five of them hovering above. "Lean over your Twisties," she said, and they both leaned over and guarded their food from the packets to their mouths.

Danny moved his towel and bag right beside Kylie and Charlie. "I think I will have a pack," he said, reaching into Charlie's bag. He pulled out a packet of Twisties and tore them open. "Watch this," he said. Then he tossed a Twistie just above his open school bag, and sure enough a seagull swooped down to grab it. But as the bird took the treat in its beak, the cat leapt out of Danny's bag–the biggest cat Kylie and Charlie had ever seen–and caught the bird in its paws in mid air, flying right through the middle of the children. Feathers flew everywhere as the cat and the seagull rolled onto the sand near the quokka, which froze in terror. There was a burst of squawking and growling before the cat got to its feet, the limp seagull in its mouth. The cat noticed the quokka and froze, staring at the furry little animal as if it were wondering if it had chosen the wrong meal. Sensing the danger, Kylie dashed in front of the quokka to protect it. The rather fearsome looking cat threw a paw out and Kylie flinched backwards, the claws only just scratching her shoulder. Then the cat turned and disappeared in the long grass on the dune, heading towards the tree line. The other seagulls had already vanished.

"Wow!" Danny said, eyes wide open with a silly smile on his face.

Far from being amused, Kylie and Charlie were horrified at what they had seen. Without a word, Kylie went straight to Miss Taylor, who was knee deep in the water, still supervising the other children. Danny watched as she pointed in his direction and explained what had happened.

"You're in for it now," Charlie said.

"Who cares? That was worth it!" Danny said, with a wicked smile on his face. "Did you see those feathers fly?"

Miss Taylor stormed over to Danny and demanded an explanation. He confirmed what Kylie had said, that he had brought a stray cat along to set it free, and it had just plucked a seagull from the sky. "And where is the cat now?"

"He went into the dunes," Danny said, "I expect he's having breakfast now. I wouldn't follow him, Miss Taylor, he gets pretty angry if you interrupt him when he's eating. I haven't fed him since yesterday, so he's pretty cranky as it is."

Miss Taylor was furious. She took Danny by the wrist and said he was going to have to explain himself to the local police. Mrs Phelps took charge of the class as Miss Taylor marched Danny up the path through the dunes. Kylie was still a bit shaken. She had never seen anything so dreadful.

"I've had a little accident," Charlie said sheepishly, looking at the wet spot in the front of his swimmers.

"Don't worry, Charlie, just go and have a swim, that'll get rid of it," Kylie said. He nodded and ran to the water before any of the others noticed. He needn't have worried as they were so busy swimming and playing, nobody had even noticed what had happened with the cat.

Kylie sat back at looked at the quokka, which was trembling. "Poor thing. Are you okay?" she asked.

"I'm fine, how about you?" the quokka said, in the most adorable voice Kylie had ever heard.

Kylie's mouth fell open. *Surely the quokka didn't really just speak,* she thought. *I must be imagining things! I must be in shock after that horrible cat incident!* "What did you say?" she asked.

"I said I'm fine. But that thing took a shot at you. Are you okay?"

"Oh my gosh, oh my goodness!" she said. "You can talk!"

"Yeah. I can also whisper. Can you?" he said with a grin.

"I must be dreaming," Kylie said, giggling.

"So you're ok?" the quokka asked.

"Yes, it's just a little scratch," she said, showing the quokka the faint claw marks on her shoulder.

"What kind of creature was that?" the quokka asked.

"That was a cat. A stray cat."

"A cat? Pooping peacocks! I've heard about cats, they're trouble!"

Just then, a flying rubber ball landed nearby. Rafa ran up to collect it.

"Hey Rafa, look! This quokka can talk!" she said. Rafa looked at the quokka, who nibbled on a blade of spinifex grass. "Come on, say something!" she said. But the quokka didn't respond in the slightest. Rafa looked at Kylie and for a second she thought she had dreamed that the quokka could talk. She blushed and Rafa smiled at her.

"Good one, Kylie," Rafa said, turning and running back to the others.

"Why didn't you say something?" she asked.

"I'm not supposed to talk to people," the quokka replied. "So I would appreciate it if you kept your voice down."

"Oh," she said.

"Can you keep it a secret?"

"Okay, I won't tell anybody...else."

"I have to go warn the others about that cat. Nice to meet you," the quokka said.

"Lovely to meet you!" Kylie said.

Then the quokka turned and hopped away. Kylie sat staring at the gorgeous creature for a moment, then got up and ran after it, soon catching up.

"I'm Kylie, by the way," she said. "Do you have a name?"

"I'm Clancy," the quokka said.

"Nice to meet you," she said.

"You too, and thanks for stepping in between me and that cat."

"You're welcome," she said.

"Even though I probably could have handled it myself. I'm no pushover, you know," the quokka said, pumping his little chest out.

"I'm sure you're not," Kylie said, finding Clancy cuter by the minute. The little creature was about half the size of the cat, and she thought it wouldn't have stood a chance.

"You know, you really shouldn't walk along talking with me," Clancy said, gesturing to her class, who were not far away, but still busy playing.

"I'll just walk with you a little way, just in case the cat comes back," she said.

Clancy stopped in his tracks and Kylie noticed his paws trembling slightly. "You think it might come back this way?"

"I'm not sure," she said. "But it certainly seemed to be interested in you. So if you like, I'll walk with you part of the way, just in case." Kylie had no idea what she could possibly do if the cat did come back, but she knew two was always better than one against a bully, and the cat was certainly a bully. And besides, she had never chatted with a quokka before and she wanted this special moment to last as long as possible.

"Well, if you really want to, I suppose that would be alright," said Clancy, looking over his shoulder. "Just don't expect me to talk if there are other people around."

"Okay, I won't, and I'll be especially quiet," Kylie said, not noticing that they had walked around a bend and were now out of sight from the class and Mrs Phelps.

Chapter 4

Miss Taylor was walking Danny along the road when she spotted a gruff, bearded ranger on a quad bike (a motorbike with four wheels). She waved him down and explained that there was a feral cat on the loose, thanks to Danny, who couldn't help sniggering. The ranger looked at him with such fury, Danny stopped breathing for a second, suddenly terrified of the big burly man. The ranger thanked Miss Taylor and said there was no need to notify the police, he would take it from here. With that he sped off on the quad bike. Miss Taylor made sure Danny knew how terribly disappointed she was with him, and how much trouble he had caused, as they hurried back to the beach. Danny felt a mix of emotions. Part of him was quite delighted that he had caused such a fuss, but another part of him hated to see Miss Taylor disappointed. After all, he was just as fond of her as the rest of the class.

When they arrived, Miss Taylor did a head count and was distressed to find Kylie was missing.

"Oh my goodness, I'm so terribly sorry!" said Mrs Phelps, who had been in charge.

Miss Taylor looked at Danny with a flash of anger, and he could tell she felt it was all his fault.

"All children out of the water now!" she called loudly–louder than the children had ever heard her speak. The class promptly obeyed. Searching the crystal clear water, she had never been so serious.

"She's definitely not in the water, or we'd see her," Mrs Phelps said.

"Has anyone seen Kylie?" she asked.

Charlie sensed a slight note of panic in her voice and wanted desperately to help. "I saw her about five minutes ago," he said, "she was sitting over there."

"Yes, I saw her too," Rafa added, "she was talking to a quokka!" This caused some giggles.

"Did you see her go anywhere?" Miss Taylor asked, ignoring the giggling.

"Um, I think she took the quokka for a walk," Rafa said. More giggles.

"Where did they go, Rafa?"

"Um, just trying to think...maybe to the lighthouse," he said.

"Are you sure?" Miss Taylor asked.

"To the ferry?" he added.

"Rafa, this is not a game! Did you see her walking, or didn't you?" Miss Taylor was becoming desperate, and the children stopped giggling.

"Yes, I really did! I just can't remember which way she went," Rafa said, his voice wavering a little, his eyes watering.

"That's okay, Rafa, thank you for helping. Alright, I need some more helpers," Miss Taylor said. And she proceeded to pick the four most responsible students: Melissa, Adrian, Charlie, and Maggie. Giving them strict instructions to call Kylie's name, to only walk for a few minutes before coming back, and to most definitely *stay out of the water*, she sent Charlie and Maggie down the beach in the direction Kylie and Clancy had taken. Melissa and Adrian were sent down the beach in the opposite direction, and she headed into the dunes, while Mrs Phelps sat with the rest of the class, including Danny.

Danny felt quite awful about Kylie. He hoped nothing bad had happened to her. Then he thought about Miss Taylor telling his parents what he had done, and his face went a ghostly pale gray. Boy was he going to get it! Probably have no TV or video games for a month. Maybe more! His parents might even decide to ban him from playing with friends. What could he possibly do to fix the situation? He watched as Miss Taylor disappeared over the dune. Then he had an idea. He jumped to his feet and ran off after Charlie.

"Danny! Come back here!" Mrs Phelps called, but he ignored her. "Danny!" she called, on her feet now. She thought about going after him, but didn't dare leave the children unattended. All she could do was watch him disappear around the bend.

He soon caught up with Charlie and Maggie and told them that they had to go back to the class, and that he was taking over. They didn't like the sound of that, especially Charlie, who didn't trust Danny one bit.

"You go back now," he said in his best grown up voice, "or Miss Taylor is going to call your parents!"

"Alright, alright!" Charlie said, believing him. He and Maggie headed back while Danny went off in search of Kylie.

Chapter 5

Now on a different beach that was several minutes walk from the lighthouse and completely deserted, Clancy didn't mind chatting with Kylie, who was keen to find out all about him. Clancy was just one year old and had a younger sister, a mother and father, and twenty six cousins, seven aunts and seven uncles, all of whom lived in what he described as "the most comfortable burrow on the island". Kylie couldn't have been more captivated.

He was equally intrigued to learn that she was an only child, and only had two cousins that she knew, the others living far away. Clancy couldn't imagine living with only his mum and dad, and wondered if she was lonely. But Kylie assured him she wasn't. Between school, dance classes and swimming lessons, she played with her cousins and the kids next door, and went to the footy with her dad sometimes, so there was never any time to be lonely or bored!

"Footy? They play that over here, the humans. I've seen them. That game is crazy! People killing each other over a ball!" Clancy said.

"Ha! They don't kill each other, they just tackle the person with the ball."

"Yeah, then they bury his head in the grass. Brutal."

Kylie was pleased that Clancy knew about her favourite sport, but thought he must be exaggerating. After all, she was one of the best footy players in her class, better than most of the boys, and she had never been hurt. "And what do you do for fun?" she asked.

"We have fun all the time! We chase each other, playfight, we go rock climbing..."

"Really? Rock climbing?"

"Yeah, sure! We don't climb very high, but we climb! Of course we go swimming, especially when it's hot. Oh, and we love surfing."

"Surfing? Oh my goodness, I *have* to see that!" Kylie said.

"Alright, I'll show you. You can surf with me, if you like!"

"Yay! I've never been surfing!"

"You're gonna love it, it's so much fun! When we get to the basin we'll go surfing, okay?"

"How much further is it?"

"See those rocks?" he said, pointing to a cluster of sunbaked rocks that stretched out into the water at the next bend.

"Yes," she said.

"It's only about two thousand hops from there," he said.

"Two thousand hops?"

"Yeah. You know," he said, demonstrating a hop, "like this."

"Oh no, that's too far. I'll have to head back now, I think," Kylie said.

"Okay. But don't you wanna see me surfing first?"

"Oh yes!" she said, excited.

"Okay, I suppose I could show you here. Let's go!" he said, and led her down to the water, the two of them walking in up to Kylie's shins, and his chest. She stood and watched in anticipation as he rubbed the sand off his front paws, then placed them in the water, looking straight down as he held them perfectly still. Then he started moving his paws up and down, like he was madly playing the piano.

"What on earth is that? You call that surfing?" she asked, smiling.

"Quiet, please," he said, focusing. She had to cover her mouth to hide her giggling, but Clancy didn't care. He was totally focused on his paws, making little waves as he moved them up and down, right and left. Soon she stopped giggling and was just wondering how to politely say she'd seen enough when she got a very nasty surprise.

"Hey!" Danny yelled, standing right behind her. She shuddered in shock and turned to see him standing over her with the meanest look she'd seen in her life. Clancy was so focused on what he was doing, he didn't seem to notice. "Everyone's worried about you!" Danny yelled.

"I'm coming back now," Kylie said.

"It's a bit late, isn't it?! Miss Taylor's already calling your mum! And she's already called the police!"

"Oh no!" Kylie said, horrified at the thought.

Clancy noticed something in the water and a big smile came over his face.

"And anyway, why did you have to tell on me for letting that cat go?!" Danny said.

"Because it killed a seagull!" Kylie snapped, her feelings changing from worry to anger, as she remembered the poor seagull.

"Yeah? Well too bad it didn't bite you instead!"

Clancy stepped onto something just below the surface of the water, then gave it a tap and it slid with him right behind Kylie, who hadn't noticed.

"I owe you for that," Danny said, and raised his clenched fist to strike. Kylie stepped backwards and tripped, landing on her bottom beside Clancy.

Danny noticed that she and Clancy were sitting on a large black object right in front of him. "Stingray!" Danny yelled.

The wings of the stingray curled out of the water, then whooshed back, and Danny turned and ran out of the water screaming.

"Sit here," Clancy said, sitting on the small hump on the stingray's back that was sticking out of the water. She sat right behind him. "Meet Razor Ray," Clancy said.

"Hi Razor Ray," Kylie said with a smile. The stingray flapped its wings in a friendly way, making little ripples in the water. "Why *Razor* Ray?"

"Coz he cuts through the water like a razor! You'll see," Clancy said, and no sooner had he finished speaking than the stingray zoomed away from the shore, Kylie and Clancy riding on its back like they were on a jet ski.

"Woo–hoo!" Clancy yelled. They picked up speed, the water rushing past them and Kylie delighted in the thrill of it. The ray slid up the front of a wave and was airborne for an exciting moment, before landing with a splash. It zipped along just below the surface, keeping its passengers above the water, then shot up the front of another wave and sailed in mid air, right beside a couple of very surprised seagulls, which squawked in fright. Kylie laughed out loud as the gulls flew off in a panic.

The stingray returned to the water with a splash, its hump just above the surface, keeping Kylie and Clancy reasonably dry, though it was impossible to avoid some of the spray from the waves. Kylie had never had so much fun!

They zoomed across the turquoise water out towards the rocky outcrop on a reef that Miss Taylor had told them was the nest of a sea eagle, known as an osprey. As they got closer, laughing and making a racket, the osprey's head popped up out of the ornate nest on top of the rocks. It looked terribly grumpy, like it had just been woken up.

"Go back to bed, Ozzie!" Clancy called out, poking his tongue out and making faces at the bird.

"Oi!" the osprey cawed back, sounding very grumpy. Two osprey chicks popped up to see what the fuss was all about. "Oi, oi, oi!" they cawed, in grumpy, high–pitched voices.

"Wow!" Kylie said, "they're beautiful."

"They're vicious predators! Sometimes they even eat baby quokkas!" Clancy said.

They were speeding along, parallel to the shore when Kylie and Clancy both saw it: the huge dorsal fin of a shark, straight ahead and coming their way. A shiver went down Kylie's spine and the little hairs on her arms stood upright.

"Flying frog farts!" Clancy exclaimed. He'd never seen a shark before, they weren't common around Rottnest. But he knew enough about them to recognise one when he saw it. He thought it must've lost its way, and was probably very hungry!

Clancy strummed his paws over the hump of the stingray, which reacted immediately, slowing down. But the shark didn't slow down, the fin climbing higher out of the water, its back becoming visible. A wave rippled through the wings of the stingray, which smacked against the water as the shark got closer. Kylie tried to scream but couldn't make a sound. She doubted a stingray was any match for a big shark and watched in horror as the shark's monstrous head lifted out of the water, jaws open, huge white teeth primed to strike. Then the stingray whipped sideways faster than ever, heading for the shore.

"Keep as low as you can," Clancy called to Kylie, who then clung to the wings of the stingray and lay like a jockey racing on horseback. Clancy lay in front of her, with his rather large bottom and his tail sticking straight up in the air. Kylie turned back to see the huge fin circling behind them, rapidly closing in. She put a hand on Clancy's behind and pushed it flat against the stingray, Clancy's knees bending. This immediately improved their aerodynamics and gave them a little extra speed, but the shark was moving even faster. Kylie's little heart was pounding extremely fast, her pulse thumping in her ears. Then she saw something ahead that gave her no comfort at all: they were headed for a rocky reef! They were either going to crash into it, or be eaten alive by the shark—or both!

Kylie turned around and saw the shark's enormous mouth opened wide enough to swallow them whole. It was the most terrifying thing she'd ever seen. The stingray's tail was dangling just over the shark's bottom teeth. Kylie faced forward, just as the stingray flew out of the water and over the reef in what seemed like slow motion. She held on tight as they flew through the air, then finally splashed into the shallow water on the other side. She turned back to see the shark doing exactly the same, its huge body taking to the air then diving into the water behind them. It sprung up to the surface a moment later and was right behind them again, the stingray's tail practically flossing its teeth! The shark surged, the whooshing water growing louder as it closed in. Its massive teeth were almost over Kylie's back now and were about to spring shut when the stingray flew out of the water again, the shark's jaws snapping the water like a giant steel trap.

The stingray landed with a splash and raced into the shallows right up onto the beach, where it skidded sideways to a halt. Kylie and Clancy watched in despair as the shark sped towards them like a torpedo. Just before it reached the shallows it turned around and disappeared under water, just the tip of its huge fin visible now. They watched as it sped towards the reef. The gigantic beast leapt out of the water and over the reef, and headed back out to sea.

The stingray rolled Kylie and Clancy off onto the soft, wet sand and they watched it slowly head out into the water, clearly exhausted.

"Ponking pelican poop!" Clancy exclaimed, "that was close!"

"I'll say!" Kylie said, trying to catch her breath as they lay looking up at the cloudless blue sky. Then Kylie rolled onto her tummy and saw something quite unnerving. It was nowhere near as scary as being chased by a great white shark, but it was certainly uncomfortable. There were about thirty quokkas gathered around her and Clancy, all sitting on their hind legs staring at the two of them, noses sniffing the air. She poked Clancy, who rolled over and got a bit of a fright. He cleared his throat, then spoke to the quokkas in a language that consisted of cute little tongue noises, *tuk tik tuck tock ook tut tut*. Clancy did plenty of gesturing at Kylie, and seemed to be desperately explaining himself. Finally, a rather large looking quokka stepped forward and walked right up to Kylie. It cleared its throat.

"Hello," the quokka said, with a much deeper voice than Clancy's, though it was still quite cute and had a warmth to it. "I am Kenneth, Clancy's father and head of our burrow."

"Hello, Kenneth, I'm Kylie, pleased to meet you," Kylie said, in her most respectful voice.

"Is it true that you risked your own life to save young Clancy from an enormous cat?"

"Well," Kylie said, a bit embarrassed, "I wouldn't say I risked my life, or that I..." she stopped, noticing Clancy, who was pleading silently with her to confirm his story. "Ah, well, yes, yes I did, I suppose."

The quokka leaned closer to her, its nostrils twitching as it sniffed at her and raised a furry eyebrow. "Are you sure?"

"Yes, really, I am. I was just a bit embarrassed to...hear you say it like that," she said.

"Embarrassed? Why would you be embarrassed of such a thing?"

"Well, I'm not really known for being brave, or strong or anything..." she said.

"Clearly, you are very modest and certainly very brave. We all saw the way you just rode that stingray out of the jaws of certain death, without so much as a squeak."

"Oh, I was...I was very scared, believe me."

"What creature wouldn't be? But you were brave. And, if what you and Clancy say is true about the cat, you are extraordinarily brave," the quokka said.

"Thank you," she said, still a bit embarrassed.

"And under those circumstances, it is acceptable that Clancy broke the Quokka Code, and spoke to you in your tongue. Of course, if it weren't true," he turned towards Clancy, looking him in the eye and lowering his voice, "Clancy would face a severe punishment."

Clancy cringed, lowering his eyes.

"Oh, it's true. It's absolutely true!" she pleaded, hoping desperately that Clancy wouldn't be punished. "But Clancy was very brave too!

He wanted to get back here as quickly as possible and warn everybody about the cat," Kylie said. "That's why we rode on the stingray, to get back quickly."

The old quokka looked at Clancy, who sheepishly smiled back.

"Yes," the older quokka said, "very well. But he has done you a disservice."

"What do you mean?"

"I mean that you have experienced something highly unusual. Something that happens once in a hundred years or more. You have communicated with a quokka. I fear the temptation to tell your kind will be almost irresistible. But you will have to keep it a secret. For if you don't, one of two things will happen: you will either be laughed at and made fun of, for a very long time; or more humans will come back here hoping to speak with us. Many more. And it will only be a matter of time before another young quokka opens his mouth to a human. And that will be the beginning of the end for us."

"Why? It might be the beginning of something very exciting," she said earnestly.

"Ha! We've been around humans long enough to know that it would be a very, very bad thing. I'm not trying to convince you, I'm just telling you the facts."

Kenneth seemed very wise and Kylie thought about his words. She imagined Danny and other kids and adults like him discovering her secret, and realised immediately that Kenneth was right.

THE CAT WALKED THROUGH the grassy dune, licking its chops. *What a delicious meal that bird had been! And so satisfying.* Normally after such a meal he would have found a comfortable place for a nap. But he was too curious about this new world, these new creatures, and wanted to investigate. He climbed up to the top of the dune and surveyed his surroundings. A few dunes away he could see some crows cawing and hopping about on the lower branches of a large pine tree. They looked easy enough to catch. He could sneak up in the undergrowth and pounce, and be sure to snatch at least one. But he wasn't very fond of crow–rather tough and dull eating. No, he was more interested in finding a furry little critter like the one he'd seen on the beach. That animal looked soft and delicious. And very easy to catch. He licked his lips again, scanning the grassy dunes and rocks that led down to the beach. Then his eyes widened in sheer excitement! Not one, but at least a few dozen of the little fluff balls were gathered down on the beach, talking to a girl. That same girl who'd been so nosey when he'd caught the seagull. And it looked like she was standing beside the same little critter he'd had his eye on before. The cat purred, a very deep and long purr, and seemed to smile, licking its whiskers.

KYLIE SAT WITH THE quokkas and listened as Kenneth decided he would have to call a meeting with the other clans to decide what should be done about the cat. He said the island's eldest quokka, an old recluse named Van Cleef, would have to be consulted. He was the only one who had ever faced a cat and survived. Kenneth was sure that Van Cleef would know what to do. So it was decided that Kenneth and some of the other adults would go and see Van Cleef at dusk.

In the meantime, Clancy introduced Kylie to his mother, a beautiful quokka with particularly long eyelashes and golden brown, sun–bleached fur. His little sister Emma, who was even smaller than Clancy, affectionately nudged her nose against Kylie's thigh like a puppy dog, and Kylie stroked her silky smooth fur, instantly falling in love with the gorgeous quokka. Clancy then introduced his best friend Cobba, a well groomed, charming looking quokka with shiny white teeth and a beautiful smile, which he seemed to be very proud of flashing. Cobba hurried aside as Kenneth approached.

Kenneth asked Kylie if she would agree to take the quokka oath, promising to never tell another person about her interaction with the quokkas.

"After the oath, you will be an honorary member of the clan, and you will always be welcome here; that is, if you are alone. We have only bestowed this special privilege to two people in our history. You will be the third, if you accept. So, would you honour us by taking the oath?"

"Oh yes, of course!" she said, unable to contain her excitement.

All the quokkas gathered around her in a semi-circle five rows deep, as she solemnly took the quokka oath.

"I, Kylie Frances, do solemnly swear to never tell another person about speaking with the quokkas of Rottnest Island," she repeated after Kenneth. As she was taking her oath, one of the older quokkas was busy weaving some bright blue and gold flowers. "I understand that if I break this promise," Kylie continued, "it will cause much hardship to the quokkas, and so I resolve to keep this promise for as long as I shall live."

The older quokka came forward with a beautiful blue and gold laurel wreath and Kenneth placed it on her head, thanking Kylie for helping Clancy and officially welcoming her to the clan. Kylie was absolutely thrilled to receive the honour and the laurel, and was a little startled by a sudden outburst of joyful cheering from all of the quokkas. The smiling creatures all moved closer to Kylie to hug and welcome her to the clan. Cobba quokka slipped right in front of her and flashed his white smile, asking "Hey, there, would you like a selfie?"

"Sorry, I don't have a camera," Kylie said, and he shrugged his shoulders and gave her a hug. Kylie met all types of quokkas, old and young, even mothers carrying tiny baby quokkas in their pouches. It was the most amazing feeling Kylie had ever felt, and she hoped desperately that it wasn't all some beautiful dream. Then she gasped, realising Miss Taylor would be worried sick. She hated to leave her new friends but when she explained her situation, they all understood and Clancy decided to show her the quickest way back. Kenneth looked her in the eyes, smiled warmly and shook her hand with both of his little paws. "Thank you, Kylie, I hope to see you again soon," he said.

"Thank you, Kenneth, me too. Goodbye for now," she said. Before she could leave, Clancy's little sister Emma ran into her arms and gave her a great big hug. It was the cuddliest hug she'd ever had, better than hugging her favourite teddy bear. Emma's beautiful big brown eyes were so kind and friendly, Kylie didn't want to let her go. But she finally did, and headed off with Clancy.

They walked through a quokka tunnel in the long yellow grass; tiny shafts of sunlight breaking through the gaps in the blades of grass that arched over their heads. Kylie had to crouch down slightly to fit. Clancy told her that quokkas all over the island built such tunnels so they could come and go to their burrows without being followed by humans. The tunnel led them out to a sandy path in the dunes and Kylie agreed they would no longer speak, just in case any people happened to pass by.

The sun was roasting hot and Kylie realised she had left her hat and backpack on the beach and gasped. Then she laughed at how she'd been through the most dangerous experience of her life, just seconds from being eaten by a shark, and the thing she was worried about now was her mother's reaction to her not wearing a hat.

Two birds, a red–capped robin and a golden whistler, flew overhead then shot back and circled them. Enchanted to see the beautiful birds chirping at Clancy, who *tuk tucked* and *clicked*, Kylie waved at them before they shot off at a great speed.

"It's been so much fun, Clancy. Do you think I'll be able to chat with you again soon?" Kylie asked, forgetting for a moment to remain silent.

"Sshh!" Clancy whispered, then stopped. Kylie stopped too and they listened. Something was approaching, brushing through the grass on the other side of the dune. They held their breath as it got nearer, not knowing what to expect. Judging from the look on Clancy's face, Kylie expected trouble.

She was relieved and delighted to discover it was Charlie, as he crashed onto the path, red faced and sweaty, despite his broad brimmed hat.

"Kylie! Where have you been?"

"Hi Charlie! Boy, am I glad to see you!" she said.

"What have you been up to? You've got everybody worried!"

"I know, I'm really sorry about that. Is everything okay?"

"Miss Taylor's a bit upset, but apart from that, everything's fine."

"Oh, that's good."

"Nice flowers," he said, looking at her laurel wreath as he handed over her backpack.

"Thanks," Kylie said, very glad to take the bottle from the side pouch and guzzle a few mouthfuls of water.

"Your shoes are inside," Charlie said.

"I don't suppose you brought my hat, Charlie?"

"No, sorry," he said.

"That's okay," she said, and sat down. She took her shoes from inside the bag and pulled them on.

A terrible screeching behind her caused Kylie and Charlie to jump. They turned to see the red–capped robin and the golden whistler hovering above, making a horrible screeching squawk at Clancy, and Kylie could see from the look on the young quokka's face that something dreadful had happened. Clancy looked at Kylie, his little front paws trembling, and she noticed a little tear roll out of one eye and down his cheek. The little marsupial scurried back down the path and disappeared down the quokka tunnel. Kylie had no idea what had happened, but she was sure it must have involved that dreadful cat.

"I'm sorry, Charlie, I have to go back for a while."

"What?"

"I won't be long. I have to go!"

"But Kylie!"

"I'm sorry!" she said turning around.

"Kylie wait!" She turned back and he held out four packets of treats for her. "Don't go hungry!"

"Thanks, Charlie," she smiled, stuffing them into her backpack before turning and running after Clancy.

"Oh, boy. Now I'm in for it!" Charlie said, and turned and headed back.

Chapter 6

Kylie arrived at the beach where she had met Clancy's clan, but the quokkas weren't anywhere to be seen. She soon found dozens of paw marks in the sand and followed them up through the dunes along a winding path to a large, natural wall of limestone. The pawprints led all the way to a small hole at the bottom of the wall–the mouth of a cave. Kylie crouched down and crawled inside. The soft sand on the ground was cool, hidden from the sun. There were holes in the rocky walls and roof above which allowed enough sunlight to enter for her to see where she was going. She followed the path until she came to a sudden drop. Huddled below in a large chamber that looked like a courtyard, were all the quokkas. Kylie noticed little tunnels in the walls and a spring of water in the middle that must have been a watering hole. Then she noticed that, though they scarcely made a sound, the quokkas all seemed to be weeping and consoling each other.

Soon she spotted Kenneth, the leader of the clan, lying on his side, surrounded by concerned quokkas, including Clancy's mum. Kylie was deeply saddened and her eyes filled with tears. *That poor, beautiful old quokka,* she thought. Kylie climbed down into the crowd of quokkas, searching the crowd for Clancy but not able to find him. Then she noticed a commotion to one side, where several quokkas were squawking and pointing up. Kylie looked up to see Clancy scaling the rock wall. Kylie thought he was looking rather awkward and she wasn't entirely surprised when he slipped and fell. She raced over and caught him, saving him from hitting the ground. His face was a picture of relief and he managed a tiny smile.

"Clancy!" his mother yelled, and he climbed out of Kylie's arms and raced over to his mother, who was comforting Clancy's wounded father, Kenneth. Kylie followed and crouched beside the little family. The old quokka had a nasty scratch on his furry chest. He was barely breathing.

"Van Cleef," Kenneth said. "Go to Van Cleef. Save your sister," he said, then closed his eyes.

Clancy and his mother sobbed and hugged the old quokka, Clancy climbing under his paw as if trying to get a final hug. Kylie was moved to tears. She had no doubt who was responsible for his injuries.

"Step back," said another quokka, the one who had made Kylie's laurel wreath. Carrying a pawful of leaves and flowers, the quokka began examining Kenneth, just as a doctor might. "He's still alive. I might be able to save him," the quokka said, and began rubbing some of the flowers and herbs together in its paws, then applying the mixture to Kenneth's wound.

"That wretched cat," Kylie said to herself.

Clancy turned to her, teary eyed, voice trembling. "It took my baby sister."

"Terrible, terrible beast," Kylie said, anger swelling inside her.

"She's still alive," Clancy said. "Emma is still alive. I'm going after her."

"No you're not! You're staying here with us," Clancy's mum said.

"You heard father," Clancy said. "I have to go after her."

"It's too dangerous," Clancy's mother said, then turned to Kylie. "Can you save her?"

"I, I don't know."

"Please. You saved Clancy. Can you save my baby?" she pleaded.

"I can try," Kylie said, surprising herself. She didn't expect those words to come from her mouth. Never before had she been asked to do something so important. It was a job for an adult, really, and she knew it. But she also knew she couldn't spare a minute going all the way back to Miss Taylor, telling her the story, then hoping Miss Taylor could find the right person for the job. By the time she'd done all that, it would probably be too late. If Emma was going to be saved, Kylie would have to do it, and right away.

And so Kylie agreed to help. "Which way did they go?"

"It took her through the star window," Clancy said, pointing up to a hole at the top of the cave wall.

Now Kylie understood why Clancy had tried to scale the wall and carefully looked it up and down. It was full of jutting bits of rock that she could use to step on and cling to. She set off carefully, but as quickly as she could, occasionally slipping on a loose rock, but finally making it safely all the way up to the star window, which led out to the dunes.

"You come back here right now!" came Clancy's mother's voice from below. Kylie looked down to see Clancy climbing after her, nervously jumping from foothold to foothold.

"Sorry, mum," Clancy called. "I won't come back till I find Emma," he said. He made it all the way up to the star window but couldn't quite pull himself over the top. Quokkas have rather small front paws, with large, heavy back legs and rather large behinds, which allows them to be excellent at hopping. However, they are not really designed for rock climbing. Kylie quickly took him by the paws and pulled him up.

"Let's go!" he said.

Kylie nodded and they set off.

Chapter 7

Kylie and Clancy emerged from the tunnel onto the dunes, where they soon found paw prints in the sand along with the trail of something being dragged. Kylie guessed it was Clancy's sister, Emma. Every now and then there were chaotic paw marks.

"She's still alive," Kylie said. "See here, it looks like she struggled to get free."

Clancy nodded and they pressed on, not saying a word. They were both still upset by what they had seen, and both very worried about Emma. Kylie had no idea what they would do if they managed to catch up with the cat. Perhaps she could throw a rock at it? Or poke it with a stick? She didn't know, and the thought of confronting the vicious animal sent shivers down her spine. But still she continued, thinking of poor Emma, who must have been positively frightened out of her wits.

After walking for sometime she began to feel a little weak and tired.

"You're turning red," Clancy said.

"Oh no!" Kylie said. "I'm getting sunburnt! Silly me!"

"Try to stay in the shade," Clancy said, and so she did, sipping from her water bottle and very grateful Charlie had thought to bring her backpack.

Before long the trail of paw prints ended, leading into thick scrub. They both searched the surroundings but were unable to find any tracks or signs of where the cat had gone.

"We'll never find her now," Clancy sniffled.

"Yes we will. Your father told you to go and see that old quokka somewhere, what was his name?"

"Van Cleef. He's a crazy old quokka, probably as dangerous as the cat."

"Really? Are you sure?"

"Nobody goes near him."

"Well, we have to try," Kylie said, feeling an obligation to follow Kenneth's instructions.

"Okay, but don't blame me if he bites you. He's not gonna be very happy to see I've spoken to you."

"We have to go, it's Emma's only chance," Kylie persisted.

"Since you put it that way... he lives up on that hill," he said, pointing his little paw over a valley and up to a hill covered in brush and trees.

"It looks like a long walk," Kylie said, feeling slightly overwhelmed by the journey ahead.

"Yeah, we'd better get a hop along," Clancy said.

"Get a hop along. I like that saying," Kylie said, perking up a little as they headed down the hillside into the valley, surrounded by tall trees and plenty of limestone rocks.

"So tell me more about this Van Cleef," Kylie said.

"I've never met him. But him and his clan have always been the warrior clan. When there's trouble, and the other clans are in danger, Van Cleef's clan is the one we turn to."

"What kind of trouble?" Kylie asked.

"A few generations back, some thoughtless people dumped a bunch of stray cats on the island, and guess what they liked to eat?"

"Quokkas?"

"Right. They liked birds and lizards as well, but I guess they liked us the most, coz we're chubby, and easy to catch. They were terrorizing the island. The Van Cleef Clan battled it out with them. I think most of the Clan died, but they got rid of those wild cats. If it weren't for the Van Cleef Clan, there would probably be no quokkas left on Rottnest Island."

Kylie nodded, intrigued. "I never imagined cats could be so dangerous."

"You don't seem afraid of them," Clancy said.

"I wouldn't say that. And that reminds me, your clan thinks I risked my life to save you. I don't feel very good about that. They've made me an honorary clan member, but they don't know the whole truth," she said, feeling a little bit guilty about her fib.

"Sure they do! You stepped in between me and that cat. That's a fact!"

"Yes, but I didn't risk my life! I've never heard of a cat killing a girl before."

"So? You could've been the first. That cat was a monster. Did you get a look at the muscles on that thing? Did you see its teeth? If that thing sunk its teeth into your neck, I wouldn't like your chances."

"Gee. I hadn't thought of it like that," she said.

"See? Don't sell yourself short, you deserve that head piece," Clancy said.

"Wow. I was never afraid of animals before. Except snakes, of course."

"Yeah, we've got plenty of those on the island."

"Really? Snakes?"

"Oh, yeah."

"Oh my goodness. I am *terrified* of snakes!"

"Good to know. I won't be waiting for you to step in if we come across a dugite," Clancy said.

"What's a dugite?" Kylie asked.

"A snake. Nasty suckers. One bite, and this quokka's a goner."

"Really?"

"Yeah. Dead as duck poo."

"Oh my gosh," she said, suddenly noticing the abundance of bushes and rocks around them that might be hiding a snake. Then she heard a branch snap behind her and almost jumped out of her skin. She turned around. Clancy had heard it too and both of them surveyed the bush, keeping perfectly still. The air was filled with distant birds singing and chirping insects.

"Come on," she said, hoping it was nothing to worry about. They continued for a little while further then heard a rustling in the leaves behind them. They turned around again.

Kylie saw the creature, camouflaged by the leaves and bushes. It was the biggest lizard she'd ever seen, about the length of a skateboard and bulging with muscles. It had sharp claws and shiny black scales lined with spots. Its mouth was wide open and it was looking straight at her.

"King skink!" whispered Clancy. "Run!" he yelled.

And with that, Kylie and Clancy ran through the valley, the king skink in pursuit. Kylie turned to see it gaining on them, its legs moving incredibly fast. She stopped, picking up a heavy stick, and turned and waved it at the skink. It skidded to a halt, looking more curious than afraid. It darted to one side, Kylie following with the stick. The reptile noticed Clancy hopping away. It gave Kylie a wide berth, zipping after the quokka at top speed. Then Kylie saw something terrifying. Over a dozen more king skinks emerged from the rocks and logs on both sides of the valley. They were completely surrounded.

One skink set eyes on her and charged at a frightening speed. Kylie swung the stick with all her might and struck the reptile in the chest, stopping it in its tracks. She turned to see another, its open mouth showing off a set of tiny razor teeth. *Whack!* She sent it flying.

Then she set off after Clancy as fast as she possibly could, jumping over lizards as they lunged at her. Clancy was climbing up towards the hilltop where he hoped the Van Cleef Clan still lived. Kylie could see the skinks closing in on him. Running faster than she ever had in her life, she caught up to Clancy as two skinks pounced. She swooped him off the ground and carried him, jumping over the two skinks as they collided into each other. Kylie sprinted up the hill, the skinks still hot on her tail. Clancy climbed up over her shoulder and into her backpack, watching the skinks as they formed a group, their legs pumping up and down like pistons in an engine.

Climbing the hill, Kylie began to slow, her muscles becoming tired. She could see the top, but it was a fair way off. As the skinks galloped closer, Clancy reached into the bottom of the backpack, feeling around for something he might be able to use as a weapon. He pulled out a big, green apple. The skinks were almost running on top of each other and looked like one huge lizard. Clancy took aim at the biggest skink, which was leading the pack. He hurled the apple as hard as he could. *Bullseye!* He hit the skink flush in the face and it fell back, taking most of the others with it. There were still a couple of skinks in pursuit, so Clancy reached into the backpack and pulled out an orange. He held it up, ready to throw. But the skinks fell back and darted away.

The hill was steep, Kylie was climbing on all fours now, still going as fast as she could, not realising the lizards had given up the chase. She finally reached the top of the hill and, clinging by her fingertips, she froze.There, staring straight at her, was the biggest king skink of the lot. "What's wrong?" Clancy asked, then looked over her shoulder. The king skink looked at him and licked its lips. Kylie couldn't do anything about it. If she let go, she would fall down the valley, back among the gang of skinks. But she couldn't just stand and watch this beast sink its teeth into Clancy.

"Go away!" she yelled at the top of her lungs. The creature cringed a little, but didn't retreat. It licked its lips again and lunged forward, mouth open, about to wrap his jaws around Clancy's face. It was just a whisker away when a tail swooped in and knocked the lizard sideways into some rocks. Kylie looked up to see an old, gruff looking quokka, standing over her. The quokka leaned back on its tail and used both of its powerful hind legs to kick the king skink off the hill, sending it tumbling into the valley below. Kylie pulled herself up onto the hilltop and Clancy jumped out of the backpack.

"Van Cleef?" Clancy asked.

"Hello, young Clancy," said the old quokka. Clancy was surprised that Van Cleef knew his name. The old warrior looked down the hill and saw the king skinks had regrouped and were once more on the climb. He walked over to a collection of boulders that were about as tall as Kylie, got behind one and rolled it towards the edge of the hill. "Give me a hand, will you?" he said, and they both pitched in. They rolled it down the hill and it struck the gang of lizards like a bowling ball pummeling into ten pins.

"Strike!" called Kylie, enjoying the victory, but Van Cleef was not impressed. Though he was shorter than Kylie, he was taller than all the other quokkas she had met. His face and chest bore old scars–claw marks and gashes long healed, but where fur no longer grew–that she was sure came from his many battles. Kylie also noticed he was missing a finger on his left paw. All of these things made him look quite ferocious.

"Come on, we'd better get a hop along before they make another run," Van Cleef said, and led them away from the slope.

Chapter 8

Kylie and Clancy followed Van Cleef into a tunnel in the grass, like the one they had taken earlier from Clancy's clan. They came to a very well-hidden cave and he invited them in. Kylie thought it was about half the size of her classroom, and very cosy. To her surprise, he offered them cushions to sit on that, despite being very old and tattered, were quite comfortable. He invited them to sip from the water that sprung up from the centre of the floor and flowed down a natural drain along the wall of the cave. With Van Cleef's permission, Kylie refilled her water bottle.

Van Cleef listened, stroking his sun-bleached orange and gray whiskers as Clancy explained what had happened, in quokka language. Kylie sat quietly, looking around the cave. She was fascinated to find it resembled a kind of museum, with all sorts of objects decorating the walls and nooks, many sitting on jutting out rocks that looked like shelves.

Her curiosity got the better of her and she got up and looked around, excited to discover that the objects seemed to be sorted into sections according to their age—just as she'd seen in the museums she'd visited. In the oldest section there were some old coats and hats that she was sure must have belonged to the early explorers of Australia; a brass compass; a world globe mounted on wooden legs; a telescope, and other objects she couldn't identify.

The next section contained things that were far more modern, though they also looked old: an Australian Army water canteen; some old maps and a pocket knife.

Most striking of all was the collection of weapons, including a pistol with a smooth wooden handle and brass fittings–like the ones Kylie had seen in pirate books; a spear; a bayonet; even an old, rusty machine gun, that she knew must have been from World War II.

"You'll have to go to the woodland to find your sister," Van Cleef finally said in English, getting Kylie's attention. She realised he probably wanted her to listen carefully.

"How do you know she's in the woodland?" Clancy asked.

"Because battle cats are nocturnal, just like us, and they like to sleep in dark places during the day."

"Battle cats?" asked Kylie.

"Wild cats, feral cats, whatever you want to call them. They live for combat, and they prefer dark places," Van Cleef said.

"But there are lots of other dark places, under rocks and in tunnels."

"Ah, but in the woodland they can stalk around in the trees at night, snacking on poor, sleeping birds. Trust me, young fellow, that's where it would have taken her."

"Do you think she's still alive?" Kylie asked.

"Hard to say. If it were hungry, it would have eaten her as soon as it got out of your burrow. But you said it had already eaten a seagull, so I would expect it to sleep for many hours after that. Sometimes they sleep all day after a big meal."

"It didn't eat her straight away," Kylie said, "we found the tracks. The cat dragged her over the dunes and into the bush."

"It'll probably keep her trapped in a cave or a hole in the ground, until it gets hungry again. They like to eat their prey alive. You'll have to hurry if you are to save her."

"Can you help us?" Clancy asked, "you and the Van Cleef Clan?"

"The Van Cleef Clan?" asked Van Cleef. "I'm all that's left of the Clan. The others were all lost to the battle cats," he said. This came as a great shock to Clancy, and deflated his hopes. "But the cats had their losses, too, and stayed away. Until now. As for me, I'm too old to help you. Still, you've got a pretty handy helper with this young girl," he said, gesturing to Kylie, who blushed a little. "Mind you, a wild cat is capable of badly wounding a child, maybe even killing one. But from what I saw with the king skinks, I would say you are capable of defending yourself."

Though she didn't dare show it, Kylie felt proud, and this time she really felt she had been brave.

Van Cleef got up and hopped over to a chest. It creaked as he opened it and leant inside, sorting through its contents. He pulled out a very old leather vest.

"Many moons ago, a Dutch navigator made this for an ancestor of mine. It will help to protect you. Perhaps your friend can help you get into it," Van Cleef said.

"I'll try. My name's Kylie, by the way."

"Glad to meet you, Kylie," said Van Cleef.

She smiled and took the leather vest, fitting it on Clancy. It was quite a tight fit and difficult to button up, especially around Clancy's tummy.

"It's shrunk over the years, I'm afraid," Van Cleef said.

She pulled the jacket firmly and Clancy let out a squeak.

"Oops, sorry!" she said, fixing the final button. It looked quite dashing, and covered Clancy's body from hips to neck.

"It's a bit hard to move," Clancy said.

"You'll get used to it," Van Cleef said. "I see you've taken an interest in my weapons collection," he said to Kylie.

"Yes, it's very impressive," Kylie said.

"You should take one. It could come in handy," he said. "But just remember, you have the most valuable weapon already."

"Apples and oranges?" asked Clancy.

"Your brains. Cats are very cunning, but humans even more so. And you will have to use all of your wits to defeat this cat."

Kylie nodded, looking over the assortment of weapons.

"Go on, take a weapon," the old quokka said.

She tried to pick up an old sword, but it was so heavy she could hardly lift it. She put it back and looked over the others, her eyes fixing on the spear.

"That weapon requires great skill and hours of practise," Van Cleef said. Next she picked up an ornate, curved knife with jewels on its handle. It looked rather dangerous. "Long enough to puncture the heart of a pirate, and certainly a cat," Van Cleef said.

"I wouldn't like to stab any animal," she said, putting it back. She came back to the old pistol with a wooden handle, brass fittings and silver barrel. "This looks interesting," she said, picking it up.

"A powerful weapon, with a thunderous blast."

Kylie noticed some old engraving on the barrel that read: *W. de Vlamingh 1696.* "Did this belong to the same Dutch navigator?"

"Indeed it did," Van Cleef said. "A kindly man; our ancestors led him right up here into this cave, to fresh water."

"Did he take the quokka oath?" Kylie asked, not sure if Van Cleef was aware that she had taken the oath, but guessing Clancy had probably explained it to him.

"Yes, just like you," said Van Cleef.

"Then I'll take this one," she said. "Not that I want to kill the cat, just frighten it."

"You may need to do more than that. Either way, the pistol is an excellent choice," he said.

"Can I have a weapon too?" Clancy asked.

"You have one. It's attached to your behind, you just don't know how to use it yet," Van Cleef said.

"My tail?" Clancy asked. Van Cleef whipped his tail into the air and flicked it with a *crack!*, just like a whip. Clancy's eyes widened in awe. He tried, but couldn't get his tail to do more than a harmless wave, let alone a *crack*.

"You'll improve with practise," Van Cleef said.

Kylie spotted an old fire extinguisher, about as big as a drink bottle, but twice as wide. "Does this still work?" she asked.

"I don't know, but you're welcome to it."

"Cats hate water, so it could be very useful," she said, taking the rather heavy extinguisher.

"Perhaps if you put it in your pack?" Van Cleef said. She took his advice and found it fitted in perfectly. Van Cleef then reached for an old slouch hat adorned with an Australian Army badge, and handed it to her. "You'd better take this too, protect you from sunburn. Unless, of course, you want to look like a rock lobster." Kylie smiled, grateful for the hat. She put the wreath in her backpack, then put the slouch hat on her head. It was too big and fell over her eyes. Van Cleef pinched the back of it, and fixed the back of the crown with a safety pin so it fitted perfectly. "Looks good," Van Cleef said, tightening the strap under her chin. He handed her the binoculars.

"You're very generous," she said, as he took the telescope and headed up a natural limestone stairway to the rocky roof of the cave.

"Come on. Let's go look over the woodland," he said. They came to a boulder that sat in a hole in the ceiling. Van Cleef pulled a wedge from under one side of the heavy rock and it rolled a few feet, creating an opening. They climbed out to a lookout and Kylie and Clancy marvelled at the panoramic views of the entire island. Van Cleef looked through the telescope then pointed to the woodland, and handed the telescope to Clancy. "That's where the cat is."

Clancy and Kylie looked over the woodland. The trees seemed to grow horizontally, almost lying down, their trunks and branches twisted from years of exposure to powerful winds. Kylie thought it looked like a creepy place, probably full of dangers.

"How are we supposed to find Emma in there?" Clancy asked despondently, "it's so big."

"Just go to the deepest, darkest place; you're sure to find the cat there. Though it might find you first."

Clancy swung his tail and managed to make a slight *crack*.

"There you go," Van Cleef said, "keep at it. Oh dear," he said in a serious tone. "You'd better go. *Now!*"

Kylie turned to see dozens of king skinks, many more than before, making their way up the hill towards them. They were moving faster than before and looked twice as fearsome. The old quokka began rolling the boulder back in place as he backed down the steps. "You're welcome to stay with me, but it'll be some time before we can leave the cave again. If you want to save your sister, take the emergency escape over by the tree," he said.

Kylie looked over to the far side of the hill top and saw an old boogie board on the ground beside a tree. She looked back just in time to see Van Cleef shutting himself in his cave.

"Be brave, young ones, Emma needs you!" Van Cleef called just before the boulder rolled shut. The little wedge jutted out at the bottom, barely visible, but keeping the boulder in place.

Some of the king skinks had already made it up to the top and were dashing towards them.

"Come on!" Kylie said, and they fled towards the boogie board. She dropped it on the sandy hillside as the hoard of king skinks scrambled onto the lookout. "Get on," she yelled, and Clancy climbed onto the board. The largest of the king skinks leapt into attack, teeth snapping, barely missing Kylie as she pushed away, sliding down the hillside.

They sped down the soft white sand at an incredible speed, the biggest king skink and several others chasing furiously. The big one raced right beside Kylie and leaned over her lap, trying to snap at Clancy. Kylie instinctively pulled the board to the left and they weaved sideways. But the king skink was soon right beside her again.

Clancy swung his tail at it, flicking it in the head. But this only seemed to madden the skink, and it shook its head and lunged. Kylie swung the boogie board straight into the big lizard's face, sending it rolling down the hill. She swung from side to side and the other king skinks backed off. Kylie and Clancy held on desperately as they picked up speed. The big king skink recovered and gave chase once again. Kylie steered the boogie board towards a small sand dune at the bottom of the hill. The big king skink was snapping at her back but when the boogie board hit the little dune, it jumped and became airborne, sailing over some more dunes and leaving the big skink behind.

Kylie and Clancy hopped off the boogie board and hastily made their way into a small valley between the dunes, keeping low and staying out of sight.

"I think we're safe from those stinkin' king skinks," Clancy said, looking over his shoulder.

"Phew," Kylie said, wiping the sweat from her forehead. They soon made it to the bushland and found a path.

Chapter 9

A bright emerald green frog, known as a motorbike frog because its call sounded like the *vroom vroom* of a motorcycle, was vrooming away on a damp patch of soil when its eyes suddenly bulged wide open and it stopped breathing, its "engine" instantly silent. Strutting through the woodland up ahead, coming the frog's way, was the cat. It was carrying something in its mouth, something small and fluffy. The motorbike frog soon recognised it was a quokka, and the cat was carrying it by the scruff of the neck.

Emma wasn't in much pain. She was carried that way by her mother when she was a baby, and although the cat's teeth were far sharper than her mother's, she was able to sidestep with her hind feet and so bear her weight most of the time.

Emma had never seen any animal like the cat, and had never felt so afraid. It was savage and powerful, and had brushed aside her father with a swipe of its claw. And here she was, in the mouth of the vicious animal, being dragged into the depths of the woodland. She had tried to shake herself free several times, but the cat's grip was too firm. What was going to become of her? Was the cat going to eat her? If it were, why hadn't it eaten her already? Perhaps it wanted to share the meal with some other cats? The thought made her hair stand on end.

The cat carried her under gnarly branches and over dead leaves that scrunched under her feet, though the cat's paws hardly made a sound.

Nearby, the golden whistler and the red–capped robin were weaving through the trees at incredible speeds in an attempt to see which bird was the fastest. They tweeted and chirped as they zipped between tree trunks, over and under branches like a couple of mini–jets, neither one able to take the lead for long before the other caught up. The robin pulled up suddenly then turned back and flew in circles. The golden whistler sensed something wasn't right and dipped its wings, turning back. The two of them whistled and chirped to each other, the robin directing the whistler's attention below, where the cat was dragging Emma along through the undergrowth. It was the most ferocious looking creature they had ever seen, but they had to try to save Emma. They chirped in agreement and the robin took a sudden nose dive, heading down at top speed.

The motorbike frog, who had been sitting perfectly still and holding its breath the whole time, began to exhale slowly, making a high–pitched *vroom* that sounded like a World War II dive–bomber plane, as it watched the robin swoop towards the cat in attack. The frog's eyes widened even more as the bird struck, pecking the back of the cat's head with a *tuk–tuk tuk!* like a machine gun, before it pulled up and flew through the branches.

The cat was alarmed and looked skywards, watching the robin as it flew up above the trees.

The frog made another dive–bombing *vroooooom* as the golden whistler made its descent, catching the cat off–guard, *tuk–tuk tuk!* at the back of its head.

The cat was furious at the audacity of these two small birds. It sat on its haunches, keeping a tight grip on Emma, its eyes on the two birds as they circled above.

They nosedived again, but saw that the cat was waiting, so they pulled up and flew low among the trees. The cat lost sight of them as they ducked into the shadows. Its ears pricked up and it could hear the birds' wings flapping, getting softer and softer as they flew further away. Then the flapping grew louder and it knew they had turned around to make another strike. It could hear them whizzing through the trees, zooming closer and closer. The hair on the cat's back stood up, its eyes widening as it stopped breathing. It could also hear the frog's *vroooom*, which got louder as the birds approached, and made the cat quite nervous.

The birds flew out like bullets from the shadows, the golden whistler leading the charge. The cat's lightning reflexes allowed it to duck the swooping bird, then strike with a swinging claw. *Thump!* It made direct contact with the robin, hitting it flush in the chest and sending the bird spiralling into a tree. It crashed in a puff of feathers and slid to the ground. The cat began towards it but the brave golden whistler swooped and struck the back of its head, *tuk–tuk tuk!* The cat sat back on its haunches again, preparing to counter–strike. But the golden whistler circled around the robin, which lay dazed on the ground.

The cat was tempted to release the quokka, take down the second bird, and have them both. But it knew a quokka in the mouth was worth at least two birds in the bush, and seeing that the golden bird was only interested in helping the robin, not in attacking, the cat set off on its way.

The golden whistler landed and flapped its wings vigorously, fanning the robin's face. The robin hopped onto its feet, ruffled its feathers and slurred its chirped speech. The golden whistler kept fanning it and seemed to reassure it. Before long the robin composed itself and the two birds took to the sky again, flying a lot slower than before.

Chapter 10

The cat finally came to a dried up old well made of gray stone and brick. Emma was flung to the left and right as the cat moved its head, inspecting the area. On the ground nearby was a rusted old metal bucket tied to the end of a equally old rope. Emma's view tilted as the cat looked up and she saw, directly above the well, a sturdy overhanging branch from a nearby tree. The cat stepped onto the stone edge, holding Emma out over the well. She dangled there, looking far below into the dark abyss, wondering what would be worse: staying with the cat, or falling into the well. Before she could decide, the cat opened its mouth and, legs flailing, she fell into the darkness, the gray walls blurring as she plummeted for what seemed like a very long time, though it was only a few seconds.

Paws outstretched, Emma braced herself for the bottom, and was relieved to be cushioned by a dense pile of leaves that had gathered over more than a century. She quickly looked herself over–she was alright. Emma looked around the well. The gray stone walls were too steep to climb. She followed them with her eyes all the way to the light at the top, where she saw the cat, whose piercing green eyes were looking right back down at her. Then it turned away, out of sight.

Feeling helpless, Emma curled into a ball and softly cried.

Chapter 11

Kylie and Clancy pushed on, determined to find Emma. They came to a quaint old one-carriage train at a very small platform. The driver sat behind the controls, reading a newspaper. Apart from the elderly couple sitting at the front, the train was empty. The tracks ran deep into the woodland.

"It would be a lot faster than walking," Kylie said. "Only trouble is, I don't have any money for a ticket."

"So we'll sneak on," Clancy said.

"That would be very naughty," Kylie said, thinking it over, "but it might be alright, seeing as it's an emergency." The train horn sounded and it began to leave the station.

"Let's get a hop along!" Clancy said.

They dashed to the back of the train, Clancy bounding like a little kangaroo. Kylie grabbed a handle at the rear and pulled herself up onto a platform at the back, then turned to lend Clancy a hand. He sprung off the ground with a little too much energy and hopped right into Kylie, who fell back onto her bottom. They giggled, crouching down, out of sight from the driver.

But they soon stopped giggling as the train accelerated, heading deeper into the shadows of the woodland. The twisted tree trunks looked cruel and wicked, some of them seemed to be reaching towards them like giant claws. So dense was the woodland, that some parts seemed to be as dark as night, even though it was almost midday, and the sky, which they could see through the treetops above, was bright blue, scarcely a cloud in sight.

The train wound its way slowly up hills, around bends and passed a lake. The two of them sat huddled silently at the back, hoping Emma was still okay, but neither one of them feeling very confident about it. Then Clancy abruptly sat up.

"What is it?" Kylie asked.

"It's Emma! I can hear her calling. We have to get off now."

"Okay," said Kylie. "Are you ready?"

Clancy nodded and she held his paw. Together they jumped off the back and tumbled down the sandy slope at the side of the track. They soon gathered themselves and Clancy's ears pricked up as he listened intently.

"This way," he said, and led Kylie deeper into the woodland. Kylie could hear a million insects and birds chirping, clicking and squeaking, but she couldn't hear anything that sounded like a quokka calling. But Clancy clearly did and hopped along at a steady pace.

Suddenly the motorbike frog hopped right in front of them. It was *vrooming* like mad and seemed to be communicating with Clancy.

"It's telling us there is a great danger up ahead, that we should go back," Clancy said.

"That means we're getting close," Kylie said.

Clancy swallowed hard and nodded. The frog gave a rapid burst of quick, excited vrooms, then leapt on its way.

"I don't hear her anymore. She's stopped."

"Are you sure?" Kylie asked.

Clancy nodded, and his eyes began to water. "We're too late," he sobbed.

"You don't know that," Kylie said.

"I can feel it," cried Clancy, "she's gone!"

"Nonsense! Why don't you try answering her call?" Kylie suggested.

"What if the cat hears? It might come for us!"

Kylie knew he had a point, but then realised they were going to have to face the vicious animal sooner or later. She swung her backpack around, wearing it on her chest, and took the nozzle of the fire extinguisher with one hand, the trigger with the other. "We'll be ready for him," she said.

"Alright," Clancy said, inspired by her courage. He took a breath, then made a very soft, subtle sound that Kylie wouldn't have noticed if she didn't see him making it. Clancy called for a few seconds, then stopped and they listened. "Did you hear her?" he asked, a slight smile on his face.

"No," Kylie said.

"She called back. She's still alive! Come on," he said, with renewed determination.

They set off through the thick, winding trees that seemed to be reaching down towards them with their twisted trunks and branches.

"Those trees are quite horrible to look at, don't you think?" Kylie said.

"I never thought about it. They just look like trees to me," Clancy said. "It's the cat I'm worried about."

"Yes, the cat," Kylie said. But it wasn't just the cat. It was the whole place. She'd never been to a park without her mum or dad, let alone dark woods. When the cool, howling wind began blowing at their backs, pushing them deeper into the woodland, it became impossible not to feel a sense of dread. Kylie tried to think about it in a positive way.

"The breeze is nice and cool," she said.

"The old Freo Doctor is in," Clancy said.

Kylie looked around, slightly confused. There wasn't anybody else around, let alone a doctor. "Who's the Freo Doctor?"

"That's what your people call the wind, isn't it? I've heard the tourists say that."

"Oh, the sea breeze. Yes," Kylie said.

"It comes in every afternoon, cools you right down," Clancy said.

"Yes, it is nice. Just what the doctor ordered, if you know what I mean."

"The ol' Freo Doctor. Trouble is, it's blowing our scent ahead of us, which means the cat will probably smell us coming."

"Ah, but he won't be expecting us to have weapons!" Kylie said.

Clancy nodded and they kept going. A little later Clancy stopped and crouched down in the grass, his nostrils twitching as he sniffed the air. Kylie crouched beside him, thinking he must have spotted danger. She looked ahead and spotted a hole in the ground.

"It's a well," she said.

Chapter 12

Kylie and Clancy crouched down over the well, looking into the darkness. Kylie could just make out the little brown furry ball on the bottom that must have been Emma. Clancy chatted with Emma in what seemed like reassuring sounds.

"How do we get her out of there," Clancy asked.

"I don't know," Kylie said. "We can't climb down, we'd never get out. There!" she said, pointing out the rope and the rusty bucket. "We'll lower it down and she can climb in!"

"That might work!" Clancy said.

A moment later Kylie was lowering the bucket and rope as Clancy stood by, offering encouragement to his sister. The bucket finally came to rest on the bottom and Clancy instructed Emma to climb in. She shook her head, terrified. Clancy spoke again, with more urgency this time, but she still refused, unable to make a sound. She pointed up.

"What's she pointing at?" Kylie asked.

"You. I think she's afraid of you," Clancy said.

"No, that's not it," Kylie said. Then Kylie looked up and there, dangling from the overhanging branch above, was a bushy, orange cat tail. Kylie and Clancy froze. The tail waved gently back and forth. Then the cat's large, orange face peered around the branch and its green eyes looked straight at them. It seemed to be smiling–a cruel, wicked smile.

Before Kylie and Clancy could respond, the cat leapt from the branch and landed perfectly on all fours beside them, the hair on its back prickling up. It hissed, baring its teeth, and Kylie gasped and dropped the rope. Clancy quivered beside her. She saw the fear on

Clancy's face and her face reddened with fury. She grabbed the nozzle of the fire hydrant as the cat hissed again, its green eyes so bright they seemed to glow. The cat looked curiously at her as Kylie took aim, gritted her teeth and pulled the trigger.

Whoosh! A wide burst of foam and water fired out of the little hydrant, blasting the cat, which let out a frightening screech. But at the same time the pressure from the extinguisher was so great, Kylie went flying backwards into the well and fell screaming all the way to the bottom.

For a moment Clancy thought the cat had fled, but when the foam and water cleared, he saw it reared up on its claws, a fearsome sight. It's back was arched, its tail standing straight up, fur soaking wet. It had the meanest, grumpiest face Clancy had ever seen. It opened its mouth and hissed at him, and Clancy responded, swinging his tail in the air and making it *crack!* But the cat wasn't the least bit frightened and leapt into attack, claws out. Clancy swung his tail around, not so much hitting the cat, but being hit by the cat as it charged into Clancy's back, sending him toppling into the well.

He landed beside Kylie and Emma on the soft bed of leaves, and rushed to his sister, giving her a big hug. She squeezed him hard, tears rolling over her chubby cheeks. Kylie gazed up to see the cat looking down at them, a triumphant expression on its soggy, wet face before it turned and walked out of sight.

"What'll we do now?" Clancy asked.

"I don't know," Kylie said, looking at the bucket and rope that had fallen beside her. "We'll have to think of something." She looked above and saw the cat had returned to the overhanging branch, its tail swinging like a pendulum as it watched over them. "Are you both okay?" she asked.

"Just some bruises, nothing serious," Clancy said, "How about you?"

Kylie noticed one of her elbows was grazed and bloody. "Nothing serious," she said.

"What's the cat up to?" Clancy asked. "Why was it keeping Emma down here?"

"Like Van Cleef said, it was still full from its last meal. Remember the seagull?"

"How could I forget?"

"So I guess it's just waiting till it's hungry again. Van Cleef said it would probably be sleepy, so hopefully we can figure out a way to escape while it takes a cat nap," said Kylie.

"I'll explain to Emma," Clancy said, and began speaking in quokka.

As Clancy and Emma chatted, Kylie investigated her surroundings. She got up and walked around the circular well, her legs sinking up to her knees in leaves with every step. She pressed her hands against the cold, rough stones on the wall, hoping for some kind of secret passage like she'd read about in adventure books. But there wasn't one. After a while she sat down beside Clancy and her lips trembled as she began to cry. She looked up at the cat, still smiling, staring at them, and that made her very angry. She stared right back, frowning and refusing to blink. Finally the cat turned away, resting its head on the branch. Winning the staring contest wouldn't help them get out, but it was a victory of sorts, and it made her feel a little bit better.

She got up and walked around again, trying to think of a way out. Lifting her feet high out of the leafy floor with each step was hard work and a bit tricky. Finally, she tripped and fell. Her hand sunk into the leaves and should have crashed into the stone wall, but kept going, beyond the wall. She realised there must have been a hole in the wall, below the leaves. She glanced at the cat, which hadn't moved and appeared to be sleeping. Then she started digging the leaves up, swishing them to one side. Clancy soon cottoned on to what she was up to and joined in, and soon they uncovered a hole in the wall. Kylie grabbed her backpack. Attached to one of the clasps was a toy with a flashlight, or torch, as Australians call it. She pulled the toy off and shone the torch into the hole.

"It's some kind of tunnel," Kylie whispered.

"Or cave. Looks pretty creepy," Clancy replied.

"Come on, let's go. Quietly," she said. Kylie climbed into the passage first. Holding the torch in front of her, she saw it was a dark passage filled with lots of nooks and crannies, and hanging with stalactites. She turned back and took Emma, placing her gently on the floor, then helped Clancy down. After handing him the torch, she then did her best to push up the leaves, almost completely concealing the hole in the wall.

Clancy inspected the torch–he'd never held one before–and shone into his own eyes. "Whoa!" he said, handing it back to Kylie. "I can't see a thing!" his voice echoing down the passage.

"Shh, not so loud," Kylie said. "You'll be alright in a minute." She took Emma's paw. "You'll have to hold on to Emma," she said, and Clancy took his sister's other paw. They slowly made their way through the dark passage.

Every now and then there were cracks in the rocks above and shafts of sunlight shone through, partly lighting up their way. The air was damp and the ground was rocky and sandy underfoot, with occasional stalagmites reaching half way up to the ceiling. When Clancy's eyes finally adjusted to the dark, he gasped and froze.

"What is it?" Kylie asked.

Clancy pointed to something that looked like a rock on the ground ahead, just outside a beam of light. Kylie shone the torch on it.

"Some kind of skull," she said.

Clancy nodded.

"A quo–?"

"Nothing!" Clancy said, cutting her off. "Nothing to worry about."

Kylie knew he was trying to keep his sister from becoming frightened, though he was frightened enough for the two of them. Kylie shone the torch around the area and saw several more skeletons that were obviously quokkas.

"Do they come down here to die?" she whispered to Clancy.

"I don't think so. Not by choice, anyway," Clancy said.

"So you think...?"

"Yes. I think this is the dining room of some kind of quokkavore."

"Quokkavore? Oh, you mean carnivore," Kylie said.

"Yes, but..."

"Oh, I get it. Oh dear. Any idea what it might be?"

"There's only one thing that I can think of. A dugite."

Kylie suddenly felt sick in the tummy. She took the old pistol from her backpack, which she was wearing on her chest again, and held the fire extinguisher nozzle in the other hand. "As soon as we see a big enough crack leading outside, we're getting out. Right?

"Right. Let's go," Clancy said, and they continued.

THE CAT WOKE, BLINKING several times and yawning while it stretched its front legs out in front then froze, mid–stretch. Looking down into the well, it couldn't see its prisoners. It blinked some more then shook its head and looked again, squinting to focus. They were definitely gone.

It leapt down from the branch and stood on the edge of the well, leaning over. No sign of them. The cat turned and looked all around, nose to the ground sniffing for a scent. Nothing. It gazed back down the well, and something caught its eye: a little hole in the wall at the bottom. The cat leant over the edge to make sure it wasn't mistaken. When it was certain, it jumped out into the middle of the well, legs stretched in front and behind, and it glided all the way down, landing quite gracefully on the leafy bottom. It went straight to the little hole in the wall, dug a few pawfuls of leaves away and found the passage. The cat stuck its head inside, holding still while its natural night–vision adjusted. Soon it could see almost perfectly in the dark passage, and it set off.

Chapter 13

Kylie, Clancy and Emma walked along as quickly and quietly as they could. They came to an intersection of three different passages.

"Which way?" Clancy asked.

"This way," Kylie said, pointing down the passage with the most light coming through the ceiling. As they wandered along, that passage seemed to have several offshoots at different stages.

"Is there a snake in here?" Emma said in an impossibly cute baby quokka voice. Clancy and Kylie stopped and turned to her.

"You can speak human!" Clancy said. Emma nodded. "How long have you been able to speak human?"

Emma shrugged her little shoulders. "So, is there?"

"We, we don't know, Emma. Maybe," said Clancy.

"So what'll we do if it finds us?"

"Kylie's got some pretty good weapons, see?" Clancy said, pointing them out. "See that one? It's a–"

"Sh!" Kylie said, keeping still again. They all heard it. It was faint, but it was definitely the sound of something sliding along the ground in the shadows nearby. Then they heard a distinct *hissss*. Kylie searched the passage with the torch and caught sight of the tip of a large, black snake tail before it disappeared beneath some rocks.

"That way!" she said, pointing down an off–shooting passage where a wide shaft of light shone from above. Their brisk walk soon became a run, and in no time they were standing around the shaft of light, looking up at the opening, which was easily wide enough for them to fit through. The problem was it was quite a way up. But the wall was made of a number of irregularly shaped rocks and stalagmites, which Kylie thought would make it possible to climb to the opening. She took the fire extinguisher out of her backpack and popped Emma inside, then climbed up over the limestone rocks. Clancy was right behind her, and soon they were standing on the highest rock, directly below the round opening. But it was just out of Kylie's reach and there were no more rocks she could use to step any higher.

"I'll put Emma out, at least she can get away," Kylie said.

"Good idea," Clancy agreed, and Kylie picked up the young quokka and stretched her hands up as far as they would go, standing on her tippy toes. But she wasn't tall enough to get Emma out through the opening.

"Jump, Emma!" Clancy called, "jump out through the hole!"

Emma hopped straight up, but still fell short. She tried a few times, each time falling back into Kylie's arms.

"Wait, I've got an idea," Clancy said, and hopped onto Kylie's back, nearly knocking her off the rock.

"Whoa!" Kylie said, "careful."

"Sorry just hang on a sec," Clancy said. He climbed up onto her shoulders. "Hoist her up!" Clancy said, and Kylie lifted Emma as high as she could. Kylie let out a tiny squeal as Clancy climbed on top of her slouch hat. "Try to hold still, Kylie," he said.

"I'm trying! I've never had a quokka on my head before!"

"Okay. I've got Emma," he said, taking his sister with both paws. "Can you hold onto me so I don't fall?" he asked.

Kylie did as he asked, holding Clancy's waist.

"Now, try to lift me, as high as you can," Clancy said. Kylie used all her strength to lift the weight of the two quokkas. When she was holding them as high as she could, Clancy held Emma up, as high as *he* could. He tried to shove her up and out through the hole, but it was no use.

Kylie's arms were getting tired and beginning to hurt. "Hurry, Clancy!" she said.

He stretched his paws to their absolute limit, but couldn't get Emma any higher. He was frustrated at being so close to the outside world, but unable to reach it. Then he saw a blue and yellow flash zip overhead. "It's Goldie and Robin!" he exclaimed. He started calling out in quokka: *tuk tuk tik tac!* He kept repeating it at a furious pace, and it occurred to Kylie that he was sending out an S.O.S.–a call for help. A slithering sound coming from the shadows nearby startled Kylie, but after looking out through the hole to the bright blue sky, her eyes were not adjusted to the dark and she couldn't see anything. She hoped like mad that whoever Clancy was signalling would come soon.

Clancy kept at it, and finally Kylie heard the frantic tweeting of two birds. She looked up to see the golden whistler and the red–capped robin hovering over the hole above, peering inside. They twitted and tweeted rapidly to Clancy, who replied with a few *tik tuk tacs*. They seemed to come to an agreement, and then each bird grabbed hold of one of Emma's little front paws. They tried to haul her out of the hole, wings fluttering at a furious pace. Emma began to lift off, but only went so far. They weren't quite strong enough to lift her all the way out.

"Keep trying!" Clancy called, "hop, Emma, hop!"

With her feet on Clancy's head, Emma hopped and the birds pulled, Clancy kept pushing, but they still couldn't get her out.

Then Clancy saw a terrifying sight: Ozzie the osprey was up in the sky above the birds and seemed to be diving into attack, claws reaching, wings stretched out wide–a terrifying sight. Clancy remembered his friend Cobba telling him that Ozzie sometimes ate little birds, and sometimes even little quokkas.

"Look out! Osprey!" he called. The golden whistler and the red–capped robin gasped, and looked behind to see Ozzie diving at full speed, straight for them. They dropped Emma's claws and vanished in a flap, just before Ozzie swooped, plucking Emma from Clancy's paws then flying away.

"Nooooo!" Clancy called, his mouth falling open in horror. His little heart sank as Emma and the osprey disappeared from view. "Emma!" he cried, but there was no sign of her. "Emma!" he cried again. He trembled and started sobbing, eyes fixed on the sky, hoping somehow Emma would come back.

Then the osprey flew back into sight, Emma in its clutches. It flew right over the hole, circling, Emma dangling just out of reach. The ferocious predator gave Clancy a few chirps, then a long, echoing whistle before flying skywards with Emma in its claws and disappearing from view.

Clancy sighed in relief and lay down on Kylie's head. "The osprey's taking Emma back to my clan," he said.

"That's great. Now we have to get ourselves out of this snake pit," Kylie said, just as she heard a raspy, scraping sound. She released Clancy and grabbed her torch, switched it on and saw, just in front of her, a huge snake on a ledge, its mouth wide open, huge fangs showing. Kylie's eyes widened in terror. The snake lunged at Clancy, wrapping its mouth around his body. He let out a squawk and swung his tail furiously, beating the side of the snake, striking one of its eyes. Kylie pulled the pistol out, aimed it straight up under the snake's scaly belly and pulled the trigger. A deafening *BANG!* accompanied a flash of fire and a puff of smoke, and the snake vanished. Clancy fell onto the ledge at Kylie's feet. She heard a slithering sound below and saw the snake sliding into a dark hole on the cave floor below.

Clancy lay clutching his tummy and moaning. "Leave me, Kylie, before the snake comes back. Please, save yourself," he said. "Tell my mum I love her," Clancy said, sounding like he was about to die. Kylie looked him over and saw that the snake's teeth had not been able to pierce the leather vest he was wearing. She checked his head and legs as he moaned in agony.

"You're okay," she said.

"It bit me," he replied.

"Yes, but it couldn't bite through the leather!"

"Huh?" He looked himself over, and was suddenly very happy and very much alive. "Pooping peacocks! I'm alive! Yippee!"

"The vest saved your life," Kylie said, helping him up.

"So did you!"

"Yes, I suppose I did."

Clancy gave her a big hug, and she hugged him back. "We have to find another way out," she said. "I can hear running water. It must lead out to the ocean." They climbed down from the ledge and back into the passage, where another fearsome sight awaited them.

Chapter 14

The cat's fur was spiked up and it was baring its teeth as it circled them, backing them into a corner. Kylie took aim with the pistol and fired again, but there was no *bang*, just a harmless *click*. She grabbed hold of the fire extinguisher and took aim. The cat flinched, expecting another soaking blast. But when she pulled the trigger, a weak stream of water drizzled out. She dumped the extinguisher and the pistol.

Desperate, Kylie searched for something she might be able to use to defend herself. Then she saw the hole nearby that the snake had slid into, and began to edge towards it.

"Slowly follow me," Kylie said to Clancy. They both moved closer to the hole. This didn't go unnoticed by the cat, who thought they must be hoping to use it as an escape tunnel. Intending to block their escape, it pounced in front of the hole. Kylie saw two tiny specks of light shining from just within the hole. *The snake's eyes*, she thought. Then the snake's black tongue darted out and touched one of the cat's hind legs, giving it a fright. The cat swung around facing the hole as the snake shot out and struck. The cat and the snake rolled along the ground, the cat screeching and sinking its teeth into the snake's throat as the reptile wrapped its tail around the cat's body.

"Let's go!" Kylie said, but Clancy was fascinated by the furious battle. Kylie grabbed him by the paw and yanked him away from the brawling animals and down the passage.

THE LITTLE TORCH BECAME faint and practically useless as Kylie and Clancy stumbled around in near complete darkness, bumping into rocks and stalagmites.

"We're going the wrong way!" Clancy said, "I think we're going deeper underground."

They stopped and listened. They couldn't hear the stream anymore.

"Let's retrace our steps," Kylie said. She held his paw and, with the torch now completely dead, they walked blindly back the way they had come. Kylie was quietly worried that they were lost, but didn't dare say it. Then she heard it.

"There! Can you hear the stream?" Kylie asked, listening.

"Yes!" Clancy said.

They took another passage and soon found the small underground stream. They followed it through the winding passage, ducking under stalactites and around stalagmites. The stream became wider and louder, and as they passed a bend, they saw it gushing down into a waterfall. Kylie and Clancy carefully walked out to the opening, incredibly relieved to see the blue sky outside and the ocean far below. For an eight year old girl and a young quokka, the waterfall was quite high–about three times Kylie's height–and the water looked very deep. Kylie didn't like the idea of jumping in. Looking up to the side of the waterfall she saw a lookout station, but to get there, they'd have to climb over steep and jagged rocks, which would be very difficult for her, and almost impossible for Clancy, she expected.

Clancy and Kylie stood silently, taking it all in, wondering what would be the safest choice: the jump, or the jagged rocks. Clancy sighed, then turned around and gasped in horror. Kylie looked back and there, coming around the bend in the passage, was the cat. It looked dreadful; fur matted and messy, one eye swollen, and walking with a limp. It hissed, and Kylie could see one of its fangs had been knocked out, making it look even more scary.

Kylie's mind raced. She pictured herself and Clancy trying to climb away, and the cat, far more agile, easily catching Clancy and doing something dreadful to him. Then she imagined them plunging into the water, the cat staying on the edge of the waterfall.

"We have to jump," she said.

"I'm not a good swimmer," Clancy said.

"Neither am I. But cats hate water, it'll never follow us. It's a short swim to the beach."

"I've never swum before in my life," Clancy said.

The cat was getting closer; growling a deep, angry growl.

"We have to jump, Clancy. I won't let you drown, I promise," she said, and took off her backpack. She zipped it up and dropped it over the fall.

"Okay," Clancy said.

"Better take off your vest," she said, and Clancy turned, allowing her to unbutton the garment, which she dropped on the ground.

The cat crouched, ready to pounce. Kylie took Clancy by the paw.

"Off we go," she said, and as the cat pounced, they both stepped backwards and fell towards the water.

The cat leapt to the edge of the waterfall and as Kylie and Clancy fell they saw it hissing furiously, just before they plunged into the cool blue water.

Kylie and Clancy kept sinking for what seemed like a very long time before they were able to kick their way up to the surface, Clancy's little paws paddling furiously. Kylie's slouch hat had come off and was floating nearby. She looked up and saw the cat still standing on the waterfall above, green eyes looking as furious as ever. Clancy, whose head kept bobbing in and out of the water, was able to grab hold of the floating backpack. But each time he climbed on top of it, the bag rolled over and he was back in the water. Kylie reached for him and Clancy grabbed hold of her arm and scrambled up onto her shoulders, his weight forcing her to go under. She kicked hard, and managed to get her head above water, despite her furry passenger. But she wasn't able to swim with Clancy clinging to her, and had to tread water. She looked up and saw the cat surveying the water. She was sure it was contemplating jumping.

"Are you alright, Clancy?"

"Yeah," Clancy said, coughing up a little water, "I'm fine."

"Good. Think you could signal the stingray?"

"Razor Ray's far from here, probably won't get the signal," Clancy said.

"You have to try, Clancy!"

"Okay, I will," he said. Sitting on her shoulders, Clancy turned around and put his paws in the water, tapping them furiously.

The cat leaned down to the water, preparing to jump.

"Please hurry, Clancy," Kylie said.

"I'm doing the best I can!" Clancy said, tapping his paws frantically.

Kylie gasped as the cat leapt from the waterfall with a *reeeoow!* that continued all the way down until it hit the water with a splash, and went under. A moment later, its soaking head appeared, looking meaner and angrier than ever.

It paddled towards them, and Kylie paddled away from it, still treading water.

"Stop moving!" Clancy said, "or I'll send the wrong coordinates!"

The cat was a surprisingly good swimmer and was approaching quickly. Kylie wondered what she would do when it got to her. She thought she would have to wrestle it away. It's razor sharp claws were ripping through the water and she feared any moment they would be ripping through her skin. Her backpack and the slouch hat were floating nearby. She grabbed the backpack and held it in front of her, hoping to use it as a shield.

Soon the cat was only an arm's lengths away from her.

"Come on, Clancy!"

As Clancy tapped out his message desperately, the cat closed in, its mouth wide open, vengeful eyes glaring at Kylie. She splashed water at it, making it cough, but not stopping it from charging through the water towards her. The cat was just a few strokes away when it lunged up out of the water into attack. It leapt right over the backpack, teeth flashing, claws primed above its head ready to come down on Kylie, who braced herself.

A sudden wave of water washed over them and swamped the cat in mid–flight, sending it backwards. The wave was caused by Razor Ray the stingray, which swept up Kylie and Clancy and swung around in a semi–circle, facing the open sea.

"My hat!" Kylie called, pointing at her slouch hat, which was floating behind them. Clancy tapped a quick message to Razor and the stingray turned back and headed for the slouch hat. They were almost there when the cat bobbed up right next to the hat. Razor slid sideways, making a sharp turn and Kylie reached for the hat. The cat sprung towards her, scratching her fingers as she snatched up the slouch hat and Razor swept her safely away from the cat.

RAZOR RAY SPED OUT into the open sea, Kylie with her bag on her back, hat on her head, and Clancy huddled in front of her. This was no pleasure ride now, in fact Razor wasn't going as fast as he had previously, and kept jerking sideways, now and then.

"Is Razor okay?" she asked.

"He seems a little off," Clancy agreed.

They heard a horrible shriek and turned to see the cat clinging to the stingray's tail. Razor jerked sideways as it tried to shake the cat off. The stingray was distressed and in pain, and the ride was getting bumpier by the second.

Kylie noticed the cat's claws digging deep into the skin of Razor's tail, causing it to bleed. The trickle of blood was dripping into the ocean and Kylie gasped, fearing that it would attract the shark. She looked to the water behind the cat and to her horror, the giant shark fin was already rising out of the water. With the cat weighing them down, the shark was soon bearing down on them.

"Oh dear," Kylie said.

Clancy leant over Kylie's shoulder, and was stunned to see the cat put paw over paw, clawing closer to the back of the stingray. When the shark's open mouth rose out of the water behind the cat, Clancy squawked in fear. He could see the shark was going to swallow not only the cat, but himself, Kylie and Razor Ray as well. Clancy leapt over Kylie's shoulder to the back of the stingray. He turned sideways towards the cat, which was almost at the base of the tail now.

The shark was right behind them, jaws wide open as the cat leapt from the tail straight at Clancy, who swung his tail as powerfully and as fast as he could. His tail struck the cat with a *crack!* and knocked the cat so hard, it flew backwards, headfirst into the mouth of the shark, which immediately dived underwater.

"Well done, Clancy!" Kylie said. Razor Ray seemed to go up a gear and carved a wing into the water, turning sharply then heading back towards Rottnest Island.

Chapter 15

The stingray sped up onto the beach. Kylie hugged its hump and Razor Ray curled both its wings over and hugged her right back. Kylie and Clancy climbed off and the stingray swam out to sea.

"Pooping peacocks, that was close!"

"I'll say!" Kylie said, putting her slouch hat back on. "That was incredibly brave, Clancy. You saved the day."

"You'd already saved it a few times, yourself, you were making me look bad," he said, and they both laughed.

"Come on, let's go see Emma," Clancy said.

BACK AT THE CAVE, CLANCY and Kylie were greeted with a hero's welcome. Emma rushed into their arms and the three of them squeezed each other in a big hug. Clancy's mother was incredibly relieved to see him, and he and Kylie were even happier to see that Kenneth was alive and looking better. He wore a bandage made of leaves and ointment over his wound, and was a bit sore, but assured them he was on the road to recovery. He asked what had happened and Clancy explained that the cat had met a horrible end and wouldn't bother them anymore. The clan was relieved and eternally grateful to the pair of heroes.

Now that it was all over, and Emma was safe, Kylie knew it was time to go. She said farewell to her new friends and crawled out of the quokka cave, Clancy by her side. Kylie gave Clancy a big hug and both had watery eyes as they said goodbye.

"Go and be with your family, I can find my way," she said. So Clancy waved and went back inside the burrow. Kylie walked through the quokka tunnel and soon emerged on the dune path.

"There she is!" called Charlie, standing beside the big, burly ranger.

"Sorry to cause you such bother," Kylie said.

"As long as you're okay," the ranger said.

"I'm fine, thanks."

"Nice hat!" Charlie said.

"That's a beauty!" the ranger agreed.

They walked back to the ranger's off–road vehicle and he drove them to the jetty, where the whole class was waiting. Everyone was so happy to see her, except Danny, of course, who seemed to be jealous of all the attention she was receiving.

"So what did you get up to, Kylie?" asked Miss Taylor.

"I wanted to catch the cat. I'm very sorry I made you all worry, that was not a very nice thing to do."

"No, it wasn't. It was a stupid thing to do," said Danny.

"Well, she wouldn't have done it if you hadn't brought that cat along in the first place," Miss Taylor said.

"Which killed at least one seagull," agreed Miss Phelps. "Talk about a silly thing to do!"

"Well, at least I'm not crazy. Kylie was talking to quokkas! She was really talking to one, even asking it questions!" Danny said.

"That's not crazy at all! I'm always talking to my dog," Mrs Phelps said.

"And it might have even spoken back to her, for all you know," Miss Taylor said.

Kylie smiled quietly as Danny crossed his arms furiously, his face red with anger.

There was a sudden commotion and Kylie noticed some of the kids were fawning over a quokka. It was Clancy's friend Cobba! Kylie almost blurted out his name, but held her tongue.

"Miss Taylor, can we take a selfie?" Kylie asked.

Cobba flashed his beautiful white teeth and Miss Taylor was smitten. "How could I possibly resist?" she said. She took out her phone and the students took turns posing with Cobba as Miss Taylor snapped away. Kylie waited till everybody had had a selfie before she took her turn. After all, she'd spent all day with a quokka.

"Smile," Miss Taylor said, and Cobba obliged, giving his most handsome smile, his eyes sparkling. He leaned close to Kylie and whispered "Clancy said to come back soon," so only she could hear. She nodded discreetly and Cobba hopped away.

The ferry ride back was uneventful, apart from the usual shenanigans from the Toohey twins. They both squeezed into a life preserver and two crew members spent most of the trip trying to get them unstuck. They succeeded eventually, only to have Sam vomit on them–he was terribly seasick.

Kylie looked back towards Rottnest Island and was a little sad to be leaving. But at the same time she felt a very warm happiness that made her body tingle. Never in her wildest dreams could she have imagined the adventures she had had, and she knew it wasn't over. Rotto wasn't far from home and it wouldn't be too long before she returned. In what seemed like no time at all she was stepping down the gangplank and into her mother's arms.

"Where did you get the slouch hat?" Kylie's mum asked.

"I found it in a cave at Rotto!"

"A cave? They didn't say anything about going in a cave. Did you stay by Miss Taylor's side?"

"Not exactly, but I was safe."

"So I take it you had a nice day?"

"The best!"

"Your father and I were thinking of going to Rotto next weekend, but I thought you might not want to go again."

"Yes, I would! There's so much to see and do at Rottnest, we didn't even cover half of it!"

"Well, that's the other thing, I think a lot of the things to do there are for older kids–like bike riding and snorkelling, that kind of thing. I was thinking we should wait another year of two."

"No, Mum. I'm ready to try those things now!"

"Well, I–"

"Mum! I'm ready. Really, I am," Kylie said, in a confident tone her mother wasn't used to hearing from her.

"Okay, so, maybe we'll go sometime soon."

"Summer's almost over, mum, we'd better get a hop along," Kylie said with a smile.

"Oh, okay...I'll organise it."

"Thanks mum, that'd be great," Kylie said, as she climbed into the back seat of the car. She took the gold and blue laurel wreath from her backpack and placed it on her lap, smiling proudly. Kylie looked out the window and could see Rottnest Island on the horizon. She kept her eyes on it as the car drove away from the docks.

THE END

**facebook.com/
jonathanmacpherson.author/
www.jfmbooks.com**

Rotto!

Book 1
Clancy the Quokka
of
Rottnest Island

Jonathan Macpherson

Chapter 1

The first rays of the morning sun shone through the hole in the roof of the cave, creating a soft light over the white sandy floor. Clancy's eyes flickered open and he rubbed them with his paw, waking up. He looked around the cave and saw all the other quokkas still fast asleep in their little corners and nooks, some of them huddled together. Clancy's mother lay on her side nearby, a little quokka nose poking out from her pouch which belonged to his baby sister, Emma, who was just a few days old. Behind his mother, Clancy's father snored in a deep sleep.

Clancy loved being the first to wake up; there was something special about it.

He leaned back onto his hind legs and stretched his front paws towards the roof high above, then hopped across the sandy floor to a small spring of water. He had a drink then took a pawful of water and washed his furry face. Wide awake now, he hopped along the edge of the stream, following it out through the entrance to a sand dune. Clancy sat back on his haunches, overlooking a stunning beach. He was only a youngster, and there was much of Rottnest Island he had not yet explored. But so far, the beach right outside his clan's cave was his very favourite place. The Basin, as the beach was known, had soft white sand and pristine turquoise water. It was flanked on the left and right by tall, rocky outcrops, which protected it from rough seas, and kept the water calm and flat most of the time.

Clancy snapped a leaf off a tree and munched on it as he hopped down the dune to the beach. He walked along the water's edge. Like most quokkas, he had never been swimming before.

"Quokkas are land creatures," his father had told him, "and unless you want to end up in a seal's belly, you'd better stay on land. Young quokkas make a perfect seal meal, I've seen it before. A little quokka frolicking in the water, then *swish!* Taken, fast as lightning. Never seen again."

This story had frightened Clancy enough to keep him out of the water, but he couldn't stay away from the beach, and loved to stroll along the water's edge. The sun was already quite warm and the water was still and so clear he could see the white sand at the bottom. It looked very inviting. He had never seen a seal, and his friend Cobba had told him seals lived on the other side of the island.

I'll just go in a little way, just get my paws wet, he thought. He looked around, checking that there weren't any other quokkas about, then Clancy waded in. The cool, refreshing water was more wonderful than he had imagined, and he was sure it would be even more wonderful if he went for a swim. *What harm could come from a little dip? The water is so clear, I'll spot a seal coming from miles away!*

Convinced it was safe, he waded out a bit deeper so the lovely water came up to his chest. *Paradise!* he thought, and ducked his head under the water. It was magical. So cool, so pleasant, like nothing he'd ever experienced. He rolled onto his back, and discovered that he could float. Paddling with his hind legs, he put his front paws behind his head and propelled himself along in the shallows. *This is the life,* he thought.

Then something under the water brushed against his back, sending fear shuddering through him. He stood up in the chest–deep water and got a fright. Lying right in front of him, just below the surface of the water, was a black stingray. Though he was relieved it wasn't a seal, he was still a bit nervous. He'd seen plenty of stingrays from the beach, but had never been up this close to one before. He had heard how stingrays could kill with their barbed tails if they felt threatened, so he decided to keep perfectly still. The ray flapped its wing–like fins, making gentle ripples in the water. It seemed to be saying hello, and Clancy thought it was only polite to reply.

"Hi there," he said, "I'm Clancy."

The stingray lifted its head above the water, its large eyes looking right at Clancy. They were friendly eyes, and they beamed in a way that Clancy was sure meant the stingray was smiling. It flapped its wings some more, then stopped as if waiting for Clancy to respond.

"How are you?" Clancy said, and the ray responded with a short burst of ripples, then stopped. Clancy put his front paws in the water and splashed up and down in a gentle rhythm, producing a similar set of ripples. Then he stopped, and it was the stingray's turn. They continued like this for a while, and Clancy was surprised to find they could understand each other, in a basic sort of way.

"Do you live in the Basin?" Clancy asked, tapping his paws in the water in a way that he hoped corresponded with his words.

The ray shook its head.

"Do you live nearby?" he asked, still tapping.

The ray nodded its head for *yes*. Then it curved its tail around and Clancy could see it had some fishing line wrapped around it.

"Want me to try and get that off?" he said, tapping his hands in the water.

The ray nodded, and Clancy gently examined the tail, unravelling the line until he came to the end, which was attached to a fish hook, pinned through the ray's skin.

"This is going to hurt. Are you sure you want me to pull it out?" he said, tapping away.

The ray nodded.

Clancy realised if he pulled the hook back out the way it came in, it would do even more damage to the ray's tail. He thought it might be less painful to pull it out the other way, so the sharp barb didn't make contact with the ray's skin. Careful not to prick himself, he pulled it through, and the ray jerked a little, reacting to the pain. But soon the worst was over, and Clancy pulled the line through, paw over paw, until he had completely removed it from the tail. The ray nuzzled its head into Clancy's tummy, like he was hugging him. Clancy patted him on the back.

"You're welcome," Clancy said.

Then the ray sprang around, facing the open water, where a seal was speeding towards them along the surface. Clancy's mouth fell open. *A seal! Here, in the Basin!* He turned and bounded out of the water. From the safety of the beach, Clancy could see the stingray zooming away in the clear, shallow water.

"Oh, no!" Clancy said, as the seal gave chase. He'd never seen creatures move so fast. The seal sped along like a torpedo, gaining on the stingray, following it out into the darker, deeper water. Then the seal circled back, bobbing in and out of the water, and Clancy realised the stingray must have got away.

"Phew," Clancy sighed, shaking his furry coat and getting most of the water off. He hopped up the dune, then looked back down to the water. The ray and the seal were nowhere to be seen, but he was sure the ray was safe.

What a morning, he thought. His first ever swim, his first meeting with a stingray, and his first terrifying encounter with a seal! *What next?*

Clancy continued up the dune when he saw a flash in the corner of his eye. He turned just in time to see something flying through the air in his direction.

END OF EXCERPT.

Rotto!

Book 3
Hunters of the Silver Plate
Jonathan Macpherson

Chapter 1

THE FERRY SPED ALONG the calm waters in the brilliant early morning sun. On the top deck, in a booth by the window, Kylie and her friend Charlie sat opposite the Toohey Twins (Sam and Sarah), looking out over the turquoise water to the island on the horizon: Rottnest Island. It had been almost a year since their class had taken a day trip to Rotto, as the island was fondly known; a year since Kylie had met Clancy the quokka, an adorable young marsupial who, to Kylie's great surprise, revealed to her a great secret: he could talk! She'd had an amazing adventure with Clancy, during which they battled a dangerous feral cat, a poisonous snake, and several other dangers in order to save Clancy's baby sister, Emma.

That adventure now seemed an awfully long time ago, and Kylie sometimes wondered if it had really happened at all, if she had truly been made an honorary member of Clancy's wonderful Clan of quokkas. Thankfully she had two reminders: her slouch hat, an old army hat that had been given to her by a wise old quokka named Van Cleef; and a laurel wreath made of blue and gold flowers that had been bestowed upon her by the Clan in recognition of her courage. In accepting her honorary membership, she had also sworn to never tell another person of her knowledge that quokkas were able to understand humans, and even communicate with them if they chose. She had kept her promise all this time, not even telling Charlie or either of her parents, and there was no doubt in her in her mind that she would continue to keep it. She was more concerned about not being able to find Clancy or the members of his clan, and not being able to continue their wonderful friendship.

She had returned to the island once with her mum and dad, but they had stayed in a chalet far from Clancy's home, and she hadn't been able to find him or any of his clan. She had tried speaking with some of the local quokkas, and even showed them her wreath, which she wore as a wristband. But none of the adorable creatures acknowledged her, apart from the customary friendly sniffs with which all quokkas great strangers. They certainly hadn't given her any indication that they understood her, or recognised the wreath.

But this time the class was headed back to Thomson Bay, which was close to where she had met originally Clancy. Kylie was sure she would be able to find Clancy this time, as the class was staying on Rottnest for three nights. *Three nights!*

It was the first school camp for Kylie's class, and everybody was terribly excited. They were a little sad not to be going with their old teacher, Miss Taylor, but their new teacher, Mr. Winston, was a nice man with a good sense of humour, and the whole class liked him.

"It doesn't work!" Sam said. He was trying to drink from his water bottle, which had an in–built straw. He raised the bottom of the bottle and sucked as hard as he could, his cheeks going red, but he couldn't seem to get a drink. Sarah had removed the lid from her bottle and was drinking from it like she would drink from a cup.

"Take the lid off," Sarah advised him.

Sam unscrewed the cap and, leaving it loose on top of the bottle, he drank from the straw. It worked, and he gave his sister the thumbs up. Then he quickly raised the bottom of the bottle to take a big swig. The lid fell off and apple juice poured out, soaking his face and shirt. Sarah burst out laughing, spraying a mouthful of apple juice all over Charlie, who was sitting directly opposite.

"Oh, no!" Charlie exclaimed, juice dripping from his glasses.

"The Toohey twins strike again!" Kylie said, and she couldn't help but giggle along with the kids at the nearby booths.

"What are you laughing at?" said Danny Wilson, the class bully who had caused so much trouble on their previous trip to Rotto. He was leaning over from the booth behind Kylie. "Think it's funny to laugh when people have accidents, do you? Maybe you'll have a little accident; then we'll see who's laughing."

Before Kylie could respond, Sam sneezed and apple juice sprayed out from his nose, causing more laughter from the kids.

Soon they had arrived and, walking off the ferry, Kylie breathed in the familiar and delightful scents of wild flowers and wattle trees. They waited outside the visitor centre as Mr Winston popped in quickly to collect keys, then they continued up to the main settlement. It was more or less like a little small town square, with a dozen or so little shops and eateries, and a number of wooden benches and tables situated conveniently beneath several trees, which provided plenty of shade. Crows cawed from the rooftops and seagulls eyed them off, hoping they might drop some food.

"Where are the quokkas?" Charlie asked, and just at that moment, as if to answer his question, two quokkas emerged from beneath a bench to greet them. Everyone was still just as taken with the adorable marsupials as they were the previous year. Like little kangaroos, only fluffier and chubbier, they were only shin high and the children knelt down to get a closer look, while Mr Winston snapped plenty of photographs.

"It's no wonder they call them the friendliest animals on earth!" said Mr. Winston, "It looks like they're actually smiling!"

Kylie searched among the quokkas for Clancy, but there was no sign of him. Perhaps Cobba was around, she thought, remembering how much he loved having his photograph taken. But he wasn't there either. A year was a long time for a nine year old and she suspected it was even longer for a quokka. *Clancy must be a grown up by now*, she thought. *He might have forgotten all about me. Maybe he's got a family of his own and is far too busy to play with a nine year old girl.*

She had looked over each of the quokkas and was feeling disappointed when a delightful aroma caught her attention. The delicious smell of baking bread, slightly sweet and somehow warm, was coming from the nearby bakery, and it seemed to have the same hypnotizing effect on everyone. Even Danny was excited.

"Can we get something from the bakery?" Danny asked.

"Please, Mr. Winston,?" several students chorused.

"A trip to Rotto wouldn't be complete without a visit to the bakery!" Mr. Winston said, and led the way inside the bakery, where the students pulled out their purses and wallets. Moments later they were sitting on the benches in the square, eating baguettes, sausage rolls, croissants and cupcakes, with the quokkas hopping around them, beneath their legs and under the benches.

"Aren't you going to talk to the quokkas, Kylie?" Danny asked, smirking.

"Oh, I already did," Kylie said, taking a bite of her deliciously warm muffin.

"Oh, really! What did they say?" Danny asked.

"They said they would..." she looked at the ground, where a quokka was pooping right next to Danny's foot. "...let their opinions be known by their actions," Kylie shaid, pointing at the quokka. The Toohey twins burst out laughing, and soon the others joined in. Red-faced with rage, Danny shooed the animal away.

"Okay, kids, let's go," said Mr Winston, wiping the eclair cream off his chin.

They gathered their things and Mr. Winston led the way up and down a winding road, shaded by branches that stretched overhead from large trees with twisting trunks. Walking parallel to the beach, they passed several bungalows that Kylie thought would have brilliant ocean views, and she wondered what their accommodation would be like. She wasn't disappointed when they arrived shortly after. The wooden cabins were surrounded by lush, leafy trees, like a small forest. The students gathered in groups of four and headed into their cabins. Kylie's bunkmates were Sarah (of the Toohey twins), Alexandra, and Maggie. Kylie climbed up onto her top bunk was delighted to see some quokkas gathered on the ground outside her window. Still, there was no sign of Clancy.

THE STUDENTS WERE LINED up, side–by–side and barefoot on the soft, white sand, facing their instructor, Colin. The young man, with blond locks and mirrored sunglasses, stood by his Stand Up board, or SUP Board, and was teaching them how to use it.

"Start by getting on your knees in the middle of the board. Paddle with the blade angled forwards, not backwards. When you're feeling confident, stand up. Okay, let's give it a go!"

They all carried their Sup boards, which were like surfboards only longer, down to the water and walked in up to their knees. Trying to get onto the board proved difficult for everybody. Charlie was the first to roll off and into the water, and this seemed to set off a chain reaction, almost everyone making a splash. Kylie almost joined them, but just managed to stay steady her board. She paddled a few strokes then carefully got to her feet. After a bit of wobbling from side to side, she managed to balance nicely, and began to pick up speed.

"Nice work!" called Colin, as she sped along in the shallows. Turning around proved to be difficult and she very nearly fell in again, but somehow managed to stay upright as she circled back to the group. The Toohey twins were surprisingly good, but everyone else seemed to be spending most of their time in the water, rather than on their boards. Danny was still on his knees and clinging on desperately to the sides of the board. Kylie noticed he kept looking into the clear blue water, and she remembered how terrified he had been of stingrays the last time they had come to Rotto.

"Step up, one foot at a time," Colin said. But Danny's hands and knees seemed to be glued to the board. Colin held onto the back of his board and gave him some more encouragement, and finally Danny lifted one knee and planted a foot on the board, then stood up, paddle in hand.

"That's it, now give it a paddle," Colin said. Danny took a few cautious paddles and before long he was gliding over the water and grinning with joy. But his grin soon disappeared when he saw the Toohey twins colliding nearby. Sam fell sideways and landed on the front end of Danny's board, thrusting it sharply into the water and catapulting Danny into the air.

"Nooooo!" Danny called, just before he plunged head first into the turquoise water. He soon emerged and scrambled onto his board, scowling. "Toohey twins!" he yelled.

Some time later, many of the students were getting the hang the hang of SUP boarding; Kylie was scooting around and manoeuvring in the shallows with ease, like she had been doing it for years. Then something caught her eye. Perched on top of a sand dune, a woman in khaki clothing and a big floppy hat was gazing through what looked like a computer box attached to a tripod. She seemed to be looking at other dunes, and taking notes in a little pad. Kylie watched her curiously for a while, then was startled by a gentle splash beside her. A stingray had surfaced and was lying on the water's surface beside her board, just floating there.

"Razor Ray?" she said quietly, making sure nobody could hear her. "Is that you?"

The ray gave her board a playful nudge, almost tipping her off, then flicked a wing and splashed her before it whooshed away. She paddled after it, excited to have bumped into her old friend. Kylie scooted across the water, following Razor as he headed out to sea. She watched in awe as Ray launched himself out of the water, flying through the air for a moment before diving back below the surface. She remembered how much fun it had been to ride on his back along with Clancy, surfing over the waves at great speed.

"Stick to the shallows!" Colin called.

Kylie stuck the paddle into the water, the sup board turning sideways like a bicycle skidding to a halt. She watched as Razor Ray continued to soar and dive into the deep water. Though she was delighted to see him again, especially as he had recognised her, she felt a bit sad to see him heading out to sea and hoped they would they would meet again soon.

IT WAS MID MORNING and Kylie and the class were assembled under a hut on the beach, where Mr. Winston introduced the children to the lady in the khaki clothes with the floppy hat: Miss Smith. She explained that she was an archaeologist and was exploring the island for historical artifacts.

"Can anybody tell me about the first Europeans to come to Rottnest Island?"

"A Dutch explorer named Willem de Vlamingh came in the sixteen hundreds," Kylie said. "He thought the quokkas were rats and so he named it Rottnest, which means rats' nest."

"That's right; he was looking for a Dutch ship that had disappeared many years before. Vlamingh spent several days here before exploring more of the coast. It was customary at the time for explorers to leave an engraved metal plate on newly discovered places, to mark their arrival. Vlamingh left plates on many islands over his voyages, but no plate has ever been found on Rottnest. I think Vlamingh might have left a plate on Rottnest Island, which remains buried somewhere beneath the dunes."

"Like a treasure?" Rafa asked.

"In a sense, yes," Miss Smith said.

"Is it a gold plate?" asked Charlie.

"The plate would most likely be made of pewter, like tin, so no, it wouldn't have great financial value. It's value would be its historical significance," she said.

"Are you going to dig up all the dunes?" asked Kylie.

"No," Miss Smith said. "I have a very powerful laser tool that can "see" through the water, the sand dunes, even the rocks, and let me see objects that have been buried for hundreds of years," she said, gesturing to the box attached to the tripod that Kylie had seen earlier. "If I detect anything that looks important, whether that be a pewter plate or any old ornaments, or even a pirate's treasure chest, I can pinpoint it and dig it up without disturbing the environment."

On a mobile computer tablet set up on a table, she showed them laser images she had taken of a cannon she said was probably hundreds of years old, buried beneath a sand dune. She had marked it for excavation and a team would be coming in to extract it from the ground, once she had finished surveying the entire island. The students were very impressed, but Kylie began to worry. Van Cleef, the old quokka who had helped Kylie and Clancy on their last adventure, lived in a cave which was full of artefacts that he and his ancestors had collected. There were tools, weapons and gadgets that spanned from the sixteenth century to World War II—it was truly an amazing collection, and Kylie had no doubt Miss Smith would find it with her laser, and take Van Cleef's collection. She had to warn him.

Her chance came after lunch, when the students had free time. Danny was eavesdropping when Mr Winston gave Kylie permission to go exploring the dunes. She set off, wearing what she hoped would make her look recognisable to her quokka friends: the wreath as a wrist band and her slouch hat. She wondered along a sandy path beneath the trees, bushes on both sides, which provided just enough cover for Danny to follow her without being noticed.

Soon, she found her way to the dunes and as she climbed up and down, she wondered if she had come the right way. It wasn't long before she came to the unmistakable wall of limestone rock, and there was no doubt in her mind now—she had come to the home of Clancy's clan.

Peering over a bush, Danny could just see the top of Kylie's head. He looked around to make sure he wasn't being followed; but when he looked back towards Kylie, she was no longer there.

Lying on the cool sand, Kylie crawled through the hole at the bottom of the limestone wall. Inside, she crawled through a narrow passage, rays of sunlight shining through the holes in the walls and ceiling, lighting her way. Kylie crawled further along and the passage became roomier and more comfortable. Soon she came to the ledge that overlooked the courtyard, where dozens of quokkas were playing, sleeping, chatting and drinking from the spring in the centre. Then, as they noticed her, a hush and stillness came over the quokkas. *Perhaps none of them recognise me*, she thought.

"Kylie!" came a voice from above, and she looked up to see Clancy, high up on the cave wall, beneath the hole they called the star window. He was clinging to one of several long tree roots that lined the wall.

"Hi, Clancy!" Kylie called. Holding onto the root, he stepped away from the rock wall and swung down and across the chamber above. There were plenty of "oohs" and "ahs" from the quokkas below as Clancy swung overhead, reached the opposite rock wall and, in one smooth motion, swapped his tree root for another, and pushed away with his powerful hind legs, swinging back over the admiring quokkas. He continued to do this, swinging all the way down to the sandy floor beside Emma, a triumphant look on his face.

"That was amazing!" Emma said, as they hugged.

"Amazingly dangerous!" said Clancy's mother, Quinby, a stern look on her beautiful face. She was a slightly graying quokka with large, curling eyelashes. "But that's that's teenagers, I suppose," she said, smiling at Kylie then giving her a hug. "Welcome back to the clan," Quinby said.

"Thank you, it's wonderful to be back."

"What took you so long?" asked Clancy.

Before she could answer, a quokka leapt into her arms and snuggled into her neck. It was Clancy's sister, Emma, and she was almost fully grown. Kenneth, the old leader of the clan, also came to greet her. He looked very well and fully recovered, Kylie thought, and you would never have known he had almost been killed when she had seen him previously. He was very pleased to see she still had her blue and gold wreath, although she had converted it to a wrist band. Clancy's best mate, Cobba, was also there to greet her, flashing his handsome smile, and pretty soon the whole quokka clan was huddled around her. Kylie was thrilled to receive such a warm welcome. After lots of hugs and hellos, they left her to chat with Clancy.

As they walked around the courtyard, Kylie told Clancy about the archaeologist she had met.

"We've had plenty of scientists come and visit," Clancy said. "They're usually very polite and try not to disturb us."

"I'm sure they are very polite, but this scientist is looking for historical things, just like the things in Van Cleef's cave. She's got some very advanced equipment, I think it's only a matter of time before she finds it."

"Do you think she'll take it all?"

"Absolutely; she'll think she's hit the jackpot!"

"We'd better go warn Van Cleef, then," Clancy said.

END OF EXCERPT.

Visit www.jfmbooks.com for cool FREE STUFF and learn more about Rottnest Island and Clancy the Quokka.

You can also visit www.facebook.com/jonathanmacpherson.author/

Follow Clancy the Quokka on Instagram @clancythequokka

Read all the books in the Rotto! series:

Book 1
Rotto! Clancy the Quokka of Rottnest Island
Book 2
Rotto! Kylie and the Quokkas of Rottnest Island
Book 3
Rotto! Hunters of the Silver Plate

How to Write a Story

I remember the first time I wrote a story. I was in grade one and the teacher asked us to write a story about anything we liked. I can't remember what the story was about, but I remember it was an action adventure story, and when I read it to the class, my classmates enjoyed it. Seeing the smiles on their faces made me want to keep writing, and I have been writing ever since.

The way I write is always the same. I try to imagine a fun or interesting character in a difficult or unusual situation. The more difficult or unusual, the better. With my story *Rotto!*, I asked "What would happen if a girl could speak to quokkas?" This was fun, since everyone loves quokkas, and wouldn't it be great if you could talk to one!?

From there, more questions followed, and my answers helped me to create or *plot* my story.

Would everybody in the story be able to speak with quokkas?

No, it would be much more interesting if it were just her secret.

Why would the quokka speak to her?

Because she did something very kind to or for the quokka.

What could she have done?

Given it food?

NO! You must not feed quokkas, it's bad for their health.

Saved its life?

Yes!

How?

Not sure.

How could a quokka's life be in danger?

Do they have any natural enemies?

Hmm.

That's when I did some *research* on quokkas. I discovered that some years ago, people used to bring pets to Rottnest Island. Some of those pets, cats and sometimes dogs, would hunt quokkas.

I did some more research and discovered that feral cats kill many native animals, and have even caused some species to become extinct!

So, my idea was: a girl saves a quokka from a feral cat, then the quokka talks to her and they become friends. I had a fun idea or *premise* for a story. Now I had to explore and develop the story.

More questions and more research followed.

Why was the girl on Rottnest Island? How did the cat get there? What kind of cat is it? What other kinds of animals live on Rottnest Island? Etc, etc.

This way I began to fill the story with different characters and situations.

But there was a really big question I needed to answer: What is the story going to be about?

Most stories involve a hero/heroine and friends going on adventure, which is usually a quest—a difficult search for something that involves overcoming many obstacles along the way. What kind of adventure could the girl and the quokka go on? What could be so important that she would decide to leave her class and set off into the Rottnest wilderness with a quokka?

I went through many options until I decided they must go on a quest to rescue a baby quokka. The feral cat could be keeping the baby quokka "hostage" for a later meal. I thought that would make a pretty good story, one I hadn't read before, so I went to work and wrote the story.

I had the main points, or plot points, which served as a kind of road map to keep me going from one incident or scene to the next. As I wrote, many other ideas came to me, and other characters and situations were created.

So that's my "process"; that's how I write stories. There are many useful books on writing, but this simple process is a good starting point and if you follow it, it could help you to write some fun stories.

The most important thing to do is to keep writing. Sometimes stories don't quite work out, and it might take a while to get the hang of it. If that happens, don't be discouraged. Just write another story. Like most things, story writing is something you get better at with practise. I also believe that the more stories you read, the better your writing will be.

I love writing stories, as there is no limit to what you can imagine and the stories often seem to have a life of their own. In other words, when you get so involved in a story, it seems very real, like the story is unfolding in your mind's eye. It's almost like you're watching a movie. It's in these moments of inspiration that you hardly notice that you are writing, and the story seems to write itself!

It's even more fun to know that other people enjoy your stories, and I love hearing from readers about *Rotto! Kylie & the Quokkas of Rottnest Island.*

You're invited to visit me at facebook.com/jonathanmacpherson.author/

and my website www.jfmbooks.com, where you can get in touch, find out more about the *Rotto!* series of books, and check out pictures of Rottnest Island and its famous quokkas. You can also sign up to my VIP Club to get FREE STUFF like my *Rotto!* Activity Booklet with colouring, puzzles and more (see cover below).

It would be awesome if you could ask your parents to help you write a review online. You can do that at the retailer where you purchased *Rotto!*

or amazon.com, and others.

Thanks very much, and happy reading and writing!

Jonathan Macpherson.

facebook.com/jonathanmacpherson.author/ www.jfmbooks.com

Made in the USA
Las Vegas, NV
29 January 2021